TERM LIMITS

STEVE POWELL

CLARET PRESS

ISBN paperback: 9781910461297

ISBN ebook: 9781910461303

A CIP catalogue record for this book is available from the British Library.

This paperback or the ebook can be ordered from all bookstores and from Claret Press, as well as eplatforms such as Amazon and ibooks.

www.claretpress.com

For Barkey

Chapter 1

Even at seventy-six, she was considered beautiful. She knew it and took pride in it. There were things she could control and things she could not. Appearance was something she could control. God had given her a lovely face and a tall, thin frame – but she kept it. She was in control.

Satisfied that she'd cleared most of the weeds, Evelyn Thompson stood. Her back was a little stiff from bending and leaning forward. An afternoon swim would loosen the sore muscles. She'd have to hurry to get that in and get back home in time to dress for the MS Fundraiser she was attending later that evening. She pushed the partially filled wheelbarrow towards the woods in the back of her property, across the back lawn. It bothered her that the cart would leave tracks on the lawn, tracks she would see as she looked out from the desk in her bedroom. The yardman mowed the lawn earlier that morning and had, as always, cut in straight lines across the length of the yard. She loved to look out, especially when the grass was freshly cut, to see things exactly in order. On its best days, the lawn looked like a fairway, with alternating stripes of light and dark green blades, one row bent towards her and the next away in near perfect order. It was part of the contrast she'd created, a perfectly maintained lawn bordered by a seemingly natural chaos of tall, brightly-colored wild flowers, five to ten feet deep around the green of the grass. From her bedroom, it all looked perfect. Except that now she could see her own tracks, marring the straight lines she demanded. At the very least, there would only be one set of wheelbarrow tracks; she'd retrace her steps on the way back from the woods.

She dumped the weeds in her usual pile and spread them, then made her way back to the detached garage. She put the wheelbarrow up against the inside wall of the garage, on its nose with the well worn handles pointing up. Then she hung the rake and put her gloves on the potting bench, spreading them so that they could dry.

She stepped back into the yard and took a moment to assess things. The azaleas against the back of the house were just over the sills of the family room windows. She had to remember to tell her yardman to trim them in the fall.

The French doors into the family room were open. The cleaning lady must have left them that way earlier, to air out the room. Evelyn slipped out of her garden shoes and, carrying them with her, stepped through the open French doors into the family room. The cool wood of the floor between the door and the area rug that covered most of the room felt nice on her hot bare feet. As she turned to close the door she saw him. By then it was too late.

He was reaching for her. His hand grabbed her hair and pulled her head quickly and forcefully back. Before she could even feel that pain in her scalp, his other hand came at her from her left. His fist held something. It was gleaming steel, a blade. Just as she recognized it for what it was, it touched her, hard and fast. She felt her skin tear. The blade seemed to run over her throat, but her throat resisted. She felt her flesh slice, again before she felt any pain. It cut through her from the left side of her neck through the harder cartilage of her windpipe. She saw the blade again, now on her right, sweeping out from under her chin. Her neck felt warm. She tried to scream. Nothing.

He stood there, tightly gripping her hair. He dropped the knife and slid his hand under her arm, holding her up until her legs started to give way. As they did, he eased her down to the floor. She watched him watch as she died.

And he did watch. His cut was deep, deeper than he imagined it would be. He thought cutting a throat would be harder. But it had been easy. Her kitchen knives must be very sharp. The life left her eyes. It didn't take long and she hadn't seemed to suffer too much. She had been much harder to select than to kill. When he was pretty sure she was dead, he simply let go of her. She collapsed onto herself and then fell off to the right.

He leaned and checked for a pulse. There was none.

Chapter 2

That night after his late dinner, Matt Mason sat on the couch in his family room. His black lab, Lucy, followed him in and settled at his feet.

He turned on CNN. The nighttime anchor was on location in Paris, reporting on a Super Power summit being held there. Mason watched TV and listened to his wife, who was talking to him from the kitchen. He was dividing his attention between each of them. The broadcast moved from the optimistic attitude of the anchor team in Paris to a scene in suburban Connecticut. Apparently the mother of a prominent US senator from Connecticut had been murdered.

Mason, a police chief, always liked to watch other small town crime scenes on the news. He tried to analyze the police department and compare their procedures to his own. Even little things like how they cordoned off crowds and dealt with the press interested him. From the looks of the dead woman's house, this PD operated in an affluent community. Mason figured they'd have great equipment. And the first thing he saw confirmed it. The patrol cars in the driveway were all new model Dodge Charger Pursuits.

He listened as the local chief made his brief statement. Evelyn Thompson, the mother of US Senator Bill Thompson, had been murdered at her home in Summerset, Connecticut. At this time, there were no suspects in custody. The report broke away from the makeshift press conference to the woman handling the story. She explained that the victim was the widow of the former governor of Connecticut and the mother of the state's senior senator. The senator was serving his fourth term and headed the powerful Senate Finance Committee.

After cutting away to show clips of the former governor and the senator, the report went back to the victim's house and the press conference. The local chief wasn't giving away much, likely because he didn't know much – the case was only a few hours old. Nonetheless the reporters kept shouting questions, trying to get more information from him, but he kept giving the same answers and assuring them that he had already told them everything he knew.

Mason thought for a moment. About three months earlier, an elderly man was found murdered in Jefferson, Pennsylvania, a town about fifty miles east of Harrison, where Mason was chief. That man's brother was a congressman from Pennsylvania. Mason didn't know all of the details of the case, but he was pretty sure that the murderer had not been caught. In fact, he didn't think they even had any solid leads. He made a mental note to check on the status of the case the next morning when he got to work.

Chapter 3

Summerset's police chief, John Mountain, knew he had his hands full. Any murder in the nationally prominent town drew a lot of attention. It was one of the wealthiest communities in the country and the media loved to provide glimpses, especially sordid glimpses, into the lives of its citizens. In this case, coverage would be at frenzied levels. His office had already received calls from the state's attorney general, who was running for governor, and from the office of the Attorney General of the United States.

Mountain hadn't had time to return either call.

He considered what he knew so far. At about 5:15 that afternoon, a friend of Mrs. Thompson, Elizabeth Berkley, stopped by to check on her. Apparently the two routinely met at the local Y to swim together. It was a loose commitment and sometimes one or the other missed the swims, so at first Mrs. Berkley hadn't been concerned. But after she'd completed her swim, Mrs. Berkley called Mrs. Thompson to make sure she was all right. She didn't get an answer on either her friend's cell or landline. She figured that Evelyn was out in her garden. She tried again about ninety minutes later. There was still no answer. A widow herself, Mrs. Berkley became concerned and decided to stop by Mrs. Thompson's house to make certain that she was okay. When she arrived at the house, everything seemed fine. The kitchen door was open with its screen door closed. Mrs. Berkley rang the doorbell and called out, but heard nothing. She let herself in. To access the backyard, she went through the kitchen and into the family room. There she found Mrs. Thompson lying dead in a pool of blood.

Several Summerset policemen arrived minutes later. They found the apparent murder weapon, a kitchen knife, beside the body in the family room. And that was everything Chief Mountain knew. There was no evidence of robbery or rape. There was simply a body and a murder weapon.

Mountain had his team canvass the neighborhood to see if anyone had seen or heard anything. Given the size and secluded, heavily-wooded nature of the properties near Mrs. Thompson's house, it was doubtful that any of the neighbors had witnessed the actual murder, but they might have seen something. One man thought he had seen Mrs. Thompson's car drive past him at about 3:15 that afternoon. He hadn't noticed who was driving. Her car, a navy blue Mercedes wagon, was not in her garage or in the driveway. The Summerset Police immediately put out an APB for the car and about forty minutes later it was found in the nearby town of Ridge. The car was parked on a busy street in Ridge, about ten minutes from the train station. Commuter trains from Ridge went into New York City approximately every sixty minutes and twice an hour during rush hour. By the time Mrs. Berkley found the body and the police found the car, as many as four different trains had gone towards New York and another six to eight east towards New Haven. And that was if Mrs. Thompson had been killed just before her scheduled swim. She might have been killed an hour or two before that. The last time anyone saw her alive was at noon, when the cleaning lady left for the day. The killer could be anywhere.

Chapter 4

He took the 4:08 local train to Grand Central.

After he'd killed Mrs. Thompson, as he walked to her car in the driveway, he peeled off the outer pair of surgical gloves that he'd worn inside the house. Once he reached her car, he removed the disposable black jumpsuit he was wearing over his street clothes. As he took each item off, he put it directly into a garbage bag that he had placed inside his backpack. Once inside, sitting in the driver's seat, he closed the door and somewhat awkwardly removed the surgical shoe covers he had on and the odor eater shoe liners he had placed inside the shoe covers. He put those in the backpack too. Then he drove her car into the nearby town of Ridge and parked on a residential street near the train station. Before he left the car, he tossed the key into the center console and adjusted the seat to its backmost position. He removed the second, inner pair of surgical gloves from his hands and carefully placed them in his backpack. Holding a sanitary wipe in his cupped hand, he opened the door and stepped out carrying his backpack. He closed the door with his hip and walked east, away from the train station. He wore khakis, a blue button-down shirt, a navy blue windbreaker, a Yankee's cap and dark sunglasses; all commonly found in stores like Walmart and Target.

He continued east for several blocks then circled around and made his way back to the station, eventually approaching from the west, the opposite direction from the victim's parked car. Using the second half of a roundtrip ticket he purchased days earlier, he took the 4:08 local to Grand Central. He got off the train in Fordham and walked to a car he parked nearby about six hours earlier. From there he drove west.

Five hours later, he made his first stop. He went to the drive-thru window of a McDonald's then pulled into the parking lot to eat. After he finished eating he dropped the second pair of inside-out surgical gloves in the half-full brown trash container in the parking lot. He gassed up and drove for another few hours. For the second stop, he pulled into an all night service center on the highway. He bought more gas and then parked. Before he went inside, he put Band Aids on the tips of his left thumb and left index finger. Then he went in and purchased three different newspapers, touching the middle one, *USA Today*, with only the covered thumb and index fingertips. Holding the papers under his left elbow, he casually slipped his left index finger and thumb into his right hand and, with a practiced motion, tugged the Band Aids free. While he waited in line at the checkout counter, he slipped the crumpled Band Aids into his pants pocket. When his turn came, holding only the outer two papers, he dropped all three onto the counter and asked for a bag. Then he went to the Wendy's inside the service area and bought a burger, a chocolate shake and a large cup of coffee. He ate in his car and read one of the papers. After he finished eating, he turned off the reading light and slipped on a fresh pair of black surgical gloves. He folded his disposable jump suit into the unread, untouched *USA Today* and disposed of it in the Wendy's trashcan next to his car. Then he dumped the entire milkshake into the trashcan, over the jumpsuit and the paper, but kept the cup.

At his next stop he tossed the backpack. During the subsequent stops he got rid of the shoe covers, the remaining latex gloves, the Band Aids and all of the fast food garbage he had accumulated along the way.

She was his fourth kill and the smoothest so far. Fourteen hours after her death, he was approaching the Indiana border. In the past five days, he hadn't really spoken to anyone other than to order meals, buy newspapers or check into and out of motels. He'd been totally unremarkable.

He pulled into a rest area and slept for a few hours.

Chapter 5

Sean Ready was the Special Agent assigned to the Thompson case. Ready was thirty-seven years old and had been with the Bureau for fourteen years. He was 6′2″ and weighed 195 pounds. He kept his hair short to make it easy to care for, and dressed like an agent: dark gray or navy suits, white shirts, subdued ties and black shoes and socks. He actually looked more imposing than he felt. Though tall and fit, he was not exceedingly strong, at least not by Bureau standards. His strength was his mind. He loved a puzzle and the more complex it was, the better.

The Thompson murder was quickly shaping up to be one of the most difficult cases he'd ever encountered. And because it was such a high profile case, it had the potential to ruin his career. Ready had plenty of successes, so there wasn't a lot of upside. If he found the killer, he was doing his job. But if he didn't, he'd quickly be replaced, presumably by someone who could.

The local chief, John Mountain, had done everything right so far but knew he was in over his head. He was also mature enough and smart enough to know he was better off away from the cameras. That was for the Feds, for Special Agent Ready.

Ready and the chief were pretty clear on how the murderer got away from the Thompson residence. Once they'd found the car, the Summerset and Ridge police had the sense to not do more than a perfunctory search. They assured the FBI's forensic team that they hadn't left any new prints or disturbed evidence. The Feds' team impounded the car and towed it away in an enclosed tow truck so that, to the extent possible, any internal or external evidence that the driver left behind might remain intact.

But after the car, there was nothing. The murderer left Mrs. Thompson's Mercedes on a residential street, so there were no closed circuit videos of him parking or exiting the car. The train station in Ridge had surveillance cameras in the station and on the platforms just outside the station, but not at the ends. The killer could have easily avoided the cameras, if he took a train. Agent Ready doubted he had; it left too much to chance. It seemed more likely he had gone to his own car. But if his car was somewhere else, presumably in Ridge, how did he get to Mrs. Thompson's house in the first place? So far, none of the neighbors remembered seeing anyone unusual around the neighborhood, though most reported seeing the usual steady stream of innocuous, largely anonymous walkers, runners and bikers. With the winding roads, the hilly wooded topography and four acre zoning, a runner or biker could easily have cut into the Thompson property unseen, from either the front or from the twenty-eight acre conservation area that abutted her land.

Agent Ready knew he had to let the local police and the field agents try to track down leads. His job wasn't to gather evidence. It was to direct the search and interpret the evidence. There was no sign of robbery. So, unless Mrs. Thompson caught an intruder right as he came in and he panicked and killed her, then left without taking anything, it seemed likely that this was something more. Who would want to kill a seventy-something year old woman? Her son, the senator? Not likely. A lover? Ready guessed it was possible. She was clearly worth a great deal of money. Maybe some gold digger had tried and failed with her. Or maybe the murder was politically motivated. By virtue of his longevity and power, Senator Thompson's name frequently came up in conversations about potential presidential candidates. Could his mother's murder somehow be tied to that? Any number of angry constituents or lobbyists or even foreign or domestic terrorists could be trying to strike out at the senator by killing his mother, a much easier target.

Ready realized he had nothing. He needed to find about more about Mrs. Thompson and her son.

Chapter 6

For the first twenty years of his life, things had gone pretty well for Greg Hopper. He grew up on Long Island, in Torrance, a middle class suburb about thirty minutes from Manhattan. Hopper's father owned a small upholstery business in Torrance. Throughout his high school years, Greg worked there, applying fabrics and picking up and delivering furniture.

An average student in high school, he was a better than average athlete. He was 6'1" and weighed about 175 pounds. He was lean and pretty strong, but mostly he was fast. And speed is one of the things you can't teach in sports. On Long Island, speed was best used in lacrosse. The coaches at the best lacrosse schools routinely tested even non-lacrosse playing freshman for speed and that was how Greg came to the sport. While many of his friends had been playing lacrosse since grammar school, Hopper had always been a baseball guy. For him it was soccer in the fall, basketball in the winter and baseball in the spring. But during his freshman year, after a soccer game in which he had played unspectacularly, he was surprised to be approached by the varsity lacrosse coach, a local legend named Howard Arnold. The kids loved him and while he was tough, he produced results. Coach Arnold asked him if he was interested in playing lacrosse. Hopper told him he didn't know how. Arnold said that with his speed, it didn't matter. All he had to do was catch the ball and run. He would be a short stick defensive middie. When Torrance was on defense, he would try to disrupt play while the opponent had possession but more importantly, once Torrance regained possession, his job was to be a short outlet for the goalie. His role was simply to catch the ball and then run like hell to the other end of the field and dump it off to an offensive middie or an attack man and then to get off the field.

Hopper made a name for himself doing just that. By the time he was a junior, colleges up and down the east coast were interested in him. He wasn't good enough to get a full ride anywhere, but his speed got him noticed by schools that his grades alone did not.

He ended up at Lehigh University, in Bethlehem, Pennsylvania. While Lehigh didn't offer him any scholarship money, the coach told him that he could participate in the school's ROTC program and play lacrosse. ROTC at Lehigh, and everywhere else, offered a full ride. Greg had actually been interested in going to West Point or the Naval Academy, but didn't have the grades, athletic talent or connections to get in, so the military service associated with ROTC didn't bother him. In fact, it appealed to him. One of his uncles had served in the Navy and, for as long as he could remember, Greg had enjoyed hearing stories of his uncle's years at sea and overseas.

Once he got to Lehigh, he adapted quickly. Between ROTC and lacrosse, he didn't have much free time, but he made the most of what little he had. He studied political science and did well enough. Unlike a lot of his more ambitious contemporaries, but like a surprising number of college students, he didn't see his education as a means to an end but as more of a rite of passage, a continuation of the directionless learning of high school. Unlike many of those less ambitious contemporaries however, he did at least have a plan: a career in the Navy, which evolved into a career in the Marines.

Originally he had planned to follow in his uncle's footsteps, but during the process of signing up he spoke with recruiting officers from both the Navy and the Marines, and Greg found the marine recruiter more compelling. He made a choice that could affect the next two decades of his life largely because he liked one man more than other.

As a freshman, being enlisted in ROTC wasn't that big of a deal. He had meetings and classes and marched with his platoon a couple of times a week, but it wasn't too taxing or time consuming. During the summer between his freshman and sophomore years, he was sent to basic training in Louisiana. It was there that he decided he'd made the right decision in joining the Marines over the Navy. For the first few weeks of basic training, all of the ROTC recruits sometimes trained together, whether they were in the Navy or the Marines. During that time, Hopper found himself more comfortable with the other recruits, officers and enlisted men who either intended to be or were Marines than he did with their naval counterparts. During the remainder of that first summer and the next summer he spent a lot of time learning things like survival skills, hand-to-hand combat and how to handle a rifle.

When he was almost finished with the second summer of training, this time at Camp LeJeune, in North Carolina, Hopper was surprised to be pulled from an afternoon fitness session to report to his platoon captain. When he got to the captain's office, Greg was met by the captain and his lieutenant. They explained that his father had passed away earlier that day, from an apparent heart attack. Hopper was granted an immediate leave and sent home to Long Island.

Greg's mother and his two younger sisters were devastated, as was Greg. While their father had never been especially fit, his death was a shock and Greg's mother was a complete wreck. On top of that, the family upholstery business couldn't run without his dad. And without the upholstery business, there was no money. The only solution was for Greg to step in and try to run the company, at least temporarily.

His father's company, Hopper Upholstery, had two types of clients: private individuals typically referred by interior designers and commercial customers, including restaurants, small businesses and regional offices of larger businesses or small hotels. While the commercial jobs were riskier, they were also much more profitable. Greg's dad had taught him the guts of the business, how to re-stuff and upholster furniture, but not his strategy. The company employed anywhere from eight to twelve people, four full-time skilled upholsterers, who knew the job better than Greg, two full-time delivery men, a receptionist/office manager and a bookkeeper. In times of heightened demand there were two or three other upholsterers and several reliable moving men who could be hired on a part time basis.

When Greg first took over the business, his main focus was

to get the existing orders out on time. There was one big order for eighty-four chairs and sixteen barstools for a new restaurant opening in a nearby town. When Greg came home after his father's death, the decorator who had given Greg's dad the job was freaking out. The restaurant furniture was scheduled to be delivered six days after his dad's death. So on top of trying to help his mother and his sisters cope and prepare for the funeral and dealing with his own grief, Greg had to somehow get the restaurant job done.

For the first day and a half he was home, he didn't even know about the order. He found out when he saw his mom crying on the phone. Cheryl, the receptionist at the upholstery company, called to say that things were falling apart and that there was this big job and the people in the shop weren't working on it, because they didn't know if they were still in business. Greg took the phone from his mother and Cheryl told him what was going on.

From his experience working for his father during high school, especially during crush times, Greg understood the pressure associated with big orders. He would come to know that the business really depended on those orders. While the profit margins on individual, residential jobs were higher, those jobs simply helped pay the employees and the bills. The real money and risk came with the commercial jobs. For some reason, with individual jobs the client or the interior decorator took the financial risk of paying for the fabric to be used in a given job. So, if someone wanted a couch reupholstered, that person and her decorator would pick and order the fabric and the decorator would pay the fabric company from the decorating company's account. The decorator would typically want to pay because the markup on the fabric was so big that he or she didn't necessarily want the client to know the true underlying costs. From the upholsterer's perspective, there was little risk involved. He simply received fabric and furniture and upholstered the furniture without any real financial exposure.

With commercial jobs, however, the situation was very different. While the client and the decorator still choose the fabric, the upholsterer sometimes paid the manufacturer for the fabric. Because of the financial risk he was taking, the upholsterer received a larger percentage of the smaller commercial markup. But if something went wrong and the client refused delivery, the upholsterer was left holding the material and was out the money he'd paid for it.

The first day at the shop, two days after his father's death, Greg only knew that he had to keep the employees on the job and get the restaurant order done. So the twenty year old took his dad's van and drove to the shop. Before he even got in the door, the restaurant's decorator and Cheryl were on him. The decorator offered half-hearted condolences, but immediately went on to say that if the job wasn't completed perfectly and on time for the grand opening, the restaurant owner would refuse delivery and Greg would be stuck holding the fabric and perhaps be sued for the restaurant's lost revenues. "Greg" would be, not the company, not his father, Greg. The business was fully his responsibility, unquestionably thrust upon him, before he even stepped inside.

He assured her it would be done – having no idea whether it could be – and stepped inside to a more compassionate, more familiar, but no less threatening reception. The employees knew and worked closely with his father, many of them for over a decade, and they cared for him and liked him. He had been a kind and fair man. And they were hugely sympathetic towards Greg, who they also knew and liked. But they were worried about their own livelihoods.

Greg decided to deal with them as honestly as he could. He told them what they already knew: the restaurant order was due in four days. He asked Bill DeNardo, the longest-serving employee at the shop, where the job stood. Bill explained that they had been pretty much on schedule, which Greg knew meant that they could have finished on time if they jammed everything through, but that they were all so devastated by the news about Greg's dad that they hadn't been able to work and weren't even sure if the family wanted them to work.

The young man gathered his thoughts and simply said he wanted to try to keep the business going. At the very least, they should complete all of the existing jobs, especially the restaurant job, so that Greg's dad could get paid, well, Greg could get paid and he in turn could pay them. He then turned to Bill specifically and said, "So let's get going on the restaurant job. You run the project. Tell me what I should do." Then to everyone else, "Let's get to work."

And they did work. All of them. They got the job done, on time and to expectations. After the furniture was delivered, Cheryl and Bill called their other clients and explained that they were still in business. They told the clients about the situation with the restaurant and encouraged each and every one to visit the restaurant, to both see that the quality of the work was as good as ever and to enjoy the great food. The restaurant's owner, glad for the many referrals, pleased with the work and legitimately grateful for the company's efforts, was in turn a great reference for Greg. Everyone simply came to believe that things were business as usual at Hopper Upholstery. And for everyone except for Greg, they were. His temporary leave of absence from Lehigh turned into full withdrawal. And given the dependence of his family on him and the fact that Greg had not begun his third year in college, the Marines gave him a full, non-conditional release without any financial or service obligation.

Chapter 7

The search efforts in Summerset provided some new evidence, but not much. There were no fingerprints on the knife and few unexplained fingerprints in the family room or in the car. They found some fabric particles in the car, but nothing extraordinary. The murderer had been meticulous. Agent Ready doubted that Mrs. Thompson's death was anything other than premeditated.

He had police and his agents search the woods in the conservation area behind Mrs. Thompson's property and that search was more productive. There was clear evidence that someone spent a considerable amount of time behind a thick stand of bushes, about thirty feet beyond the perimeter of the Thompson property. The spot provided cover and a clear view of the back and driveway side of Mrs. Thompson's house. There were several sets of tracks from the road on the other side of the conservation area to the spot behind the bushes. While the tracks all led to and from the same spot, the shoe sizes and types and the ages of the tracks were different. Either three different people came to the area at different times or one clever individual came three times, wearing different kinds of shoes of different sizes.

Agent Ready became increasingly sure that whoever killed Mrs. Thompson had planned it very carefully. He had to learn more about her and her son to figure out who their enemies might be.

Chapter 8

The morning after seeing the news of the murder of the elderly woman in Connecticut, the senator's mother, Matt Mason intended to check out the status of the investigation into the murder of the congressman's brother in central Pennsylvania. But on his way to the station, he was called to the scene of a fender bender involving the town's mayor. His day went downhill from there. It would be a few more days before he got around to looking into the status of the congressman's brother's murder.

Chapter 9

For the next few years, Greg simply worked. The goodwill that his father had created over the years and the good name that Greg and the team built with their diligent work following his father's death kept the business going for the first few months after Greg took over. However, while they were able to win new orders for small projects, they were hard pressed to win critical commercial orders. Businesses simply weren't willing to risk missing a crucial opening deadline on a twenty year old. Greg needed someone older to add credibility. He considered bringing in Bill DeNardo, the longest employed upholsterer, as a partner, but he and his mother and sisters needed every penny of the company's already sparse profits. So instead, he brought in his mother. She was forty-three years old and an attractive, personable, smart woman. And she was lost without her husband. Greg thought that partnering with her would solve the business's maturity problem and give her something to focus on other than her grief.

His plan worked beautifully. Greg ran the company on a day-to-day basis while his mother took care of his younger sisters. She came into the office for an hour or two every day or when she was needed to win a client or hold one's hand. Together, they were very effective. Greg came into his own running the business and within a couple of years, decorators on Long Island knew Hopper Upholstery was still a reliable, quality upholsterer.

For his part, Greg enjoyed running the company and working with his mother. She was grateful to be needed and quickly adapted to her role as the company's mature public face. She liked working with clients and was a good sounding board for her son's ideas. And Greg did have ideas. First he wanted to try to get more business in Manhattan. While his transportation costs were moderately higher than those of the Manhattan firms, the rent for his space was a fraction of theirs. On top of that, he found a new, much bigger space about twenty minutes further out on the island. While the bigger space cost more, they could house more skilled upholsterers, hold more product and do more and bigger jobs.

It took a while, but eventually Greg convinced his mom to go along with it. With the two of them running the business for three years and with their finances in good order, in part from the proceeds of Greg's father's life insurance, they were able to secure a lease on the property Greg wanted. Greg and his mom then went after the decorators who were the lifeline of their business. Most of those decorators were Long Island based, but did the vast majority of their fabric shopping in Manhattan at the Decorators & Design Building and at the fabric houses' showrooms. Greg induced the decorators he did business with to encourage their decorator friends in Manhattan to use Hopper Upholstery by offering to reduce the prices he charged Long Island decorators for any referrals and by undercutting the prices of his own Manhattan competitors. Gradually, his plan worked. Initially he won mostly individual jobs, but he used those as loss leaders and always went the extra mile to insure that his company's work was of the highest quality and delivered on time. The decorators who tested him out with retail clients started to use him for smaller commercial projects and, when those panned out, they gave him slightly bigger jobs. Within a couple of years, it was clear that the expansion had paid off.

Chapter 10

From the rest stop in Indiana, he drove north to Ann Arbor, Michigan. In Ann Arbor, he got a room at a Best Western just outside the city and rested for a few days, reading papers and watching the news. The murder in Summerset was still a focal point, but it was fading fast. He had mixed emotions about that. On the one hand, while the local police and the FBI claimed they were following leads, the consensus among reporters was that they didn't seem to really have any. So it appeared that he had gotten away with it again, at least for now. On the other hand, no one had yet seen the pattern. His message wasn't getting out.

The next morning, he took his car to a brushless car wash and had it thoroughly cleaned, inside and out. When one of the attendants asked why he was washing a rental car, he explained that it was an Enterprise long-term rental, and that he had it for another couple of weeks and couldn't stand the mess.

From there, he checked out of his hotel and drove to the parking lot of a large shopping center. He wiped down the inside of the car and returned it to Enterprise. Then he took a bus to Detroit and a train from there to Denver.

Chapter 11

Four days after Mrs. Thompson's murder, Chief Mason finally had some free time. He logged into the computer in his office and googled the name Doug Boeckh. There were pages of results. He clicked on the first two.

Douglas James Boeckh, born April 17, 1937, died March 11, 2014. Brother of Congressman John Boeckh, (7th District, Pennsylvania)...

Doug Boeckh was found murdered in his home on March 11, 2014. While local police say they are pursuing leads...

There wasn't much there. Mason scanned through several more articles. It seemed that the deceased Mr. Boeckh had been a frequent source of embarrassment for his congressman brother. He had a drunk driving conviction and was alleged to have had a problem with gambling. He was murdered in his own home, with his own letter opener, stabbed through the ear. The letter opener was a gift from his brother. Its handle was enamel with a congressional seal.

Mason considered the two murders. Each victim was a relative of a nationally known politician. The chief knew that Boeckh had been a congressman forever. He looked online and saw that he had been elected 19 times and was in his 39th year in Congress. Boeckh was the longest-serving congressman or senator in Pennsylvania. It struck Mason that Senator Thompson had been around for a long time too. Just as he was about to look it up, his phone rang.

Chapter 12

One day when Hopper was about twenty-three, he was filling in for one of his delivery drivers, dropping off a couch for a woman who lived in Torrance. The woman was an acquaintance of his mother and Greg wanted to be sure she was happy or he knew he'd hear about it later.

He pulled the truck into her driveway and went up to her front door, to make sure she was home before he unloaded the couch. He rang the doorbell and waited. From inside the house he heard a woman's voice say, "I'll get it, Mom."

Then he heard footsteps and the door opened.

At first, he didn't say anything. He just stood, staring.

The beautiful woman he was staring at smiled and then laughed. "Greg Hopper, aren't you even going to say hello?"

Now Hopper really felt stupid. Not only had he been looking at this stunning woman with, he was sure, an open-mouthed, awestruck, stupid expression on his face, but he was too shocked to even speak, and to make matters worse, she seemed to know him. He had no idea who she was.

She was gorgeous. About 5'7", maybe 5'8", her body was perfect. She wore jeans, a tee shirt and a pair of sneakers. Even dressed casually, she was breathtaking. She had wavy blondish brown hair that came to about her shoulders, and the most incredible face. It wasn't at all fat, but it was full, especially her cheeks. And when she smiled her whole face smiled, her blue eyes, her mouth, even her cheeks. He tried not to stare, but he couldn't seem to stop. She was so pretty.

Finally he managed to speak. His first brilliant words were, "Um, hi." And even his "hi" came out as more of a question than a greeting.

She laughed again. It was an honest laugh, not at all mean or arrogant. "You don't remember me, do you?"

He looked at her face and then down her body to her feet, as if scanning her would somehow help him to identify her. God she was amazing. When he got back up to her eyes, he could see her delight in his complete befuddlement.

"I'm Sarah, Sarah Jennings."

His mind raced. She must be Mrs. Jennings' daughter. Her name was still Jennings, so at least she wasn't married. He tried to figure out her age. She could have been any where from eighteen to twenty-eight.

"Who's at the door, Sarah?"

The new voice was accompanied by the sound of footsteps. Mrs. Jennings came into the front hall. He did recognize her.

"Oh, hi Greg. Right on time. How are you, dear?"

Her daughter turned from her mother back to Greg, still grinning at him. He looked from her back to her mother. Finally he opened his mouth.

"Hi, Mrs. Jennings. It's nice to see you, ma'am."

"Greg, do you remember my daughter, Sarah? She went to Torrance High with you."

Greg's face looked confused again. Surely he would remember her if they had been in high school together.

Sarah finally showed some mercy and turned to her mother. "Greg wouldn't remember me, Mom. I was just a freshman when he was a senior."

Mrs. Jennings could hear the teasing tone in her daughter's voice and was no doubt used to the effect her appearance had on men. She smiled and said, "Well then, it's time you met. Greg, this is my daughter Sarah. She's a junior at Fordham."

She turned to her daughter. "Greg took over his father's business a couple of years ago." Then, remembering the circumstances behind everything, she turned back to Greg. "I'm so sorry about your dad, Greg. He was a very nice man. I didn't know him well, but he was always so kind."

Finally he was able to speak with a voice. He had heard a lot of sympathy over the past few years and could tell the difference between platitudes and sincerity. Mrs. Jennings was sincere. "Thank you, Mrs. Jennings. You're very nice to say so."

She turned back to her daughter and said, "Greg's dad, Mr. Hopper, passed away suddenly two or three years ago. Greg took over the business for him." Her tone was full of admiration. She turned back to him. "You were in college at the time, weren't you?"

"Yes, ma'am. At Lehigh."

Sarah spoke next. "I heard about your dad, Greg. I'm so sorry." She extended her hand and smiled, lightening things instantly. "It's nice to meet you."

He smiled, too. He reached out and took her hand in his. Her skin was soft, her hands were thin and her grip was nice, just perfect. He would remember the feeling of touching her that first time for the rest of his life. Then he actually spoke to her, confidently. Seeing the mischief at his earlier awkwardness back in her gleaming eyes, he smiled back, almost laughing. "It's nice to meet you, too."

She held her fingers around his hand, letting them linger there.

Mrs. Jennings, who was oblivious to the little moment that was going on in front of her, interjected. "The new couch goes in the family room. I was wondering if you wouldn't mind moving the old one down into the basement for me. Sarah and I were going to try, but I didn't think we could handle it."

"Of course. Mike, my associate, is out in the truck. He and I will do that. We should do it first, to make room. Maybe you could show me where you want everything and the path you want us to use through your house?" He bent to untie his shoes.

"Don't worry about your shoes. Come on. I'll show you."

As she showed him what she wanted done, Greg wondered whether her husband was out of the picture. He'd have to ask his mom what the deal was. Maybe she was a widow, too. That would explain the heartfelt sympathy that she and her daughter seemed to feel.

Twenty minutes later, the old couch was in the basement and the new one was in place in the family room. Sarah and her mom both seemed pleased.

Chapter 13

Ten days after Mrs. Thompson's murder, FBI Agent Sean Ready was no closer to solving the case than he had been on the first day.

Mrs. Thompson's son, the senator, seemed an unlikely suspect. He was in Washington on the day of the murder, so at the very least he didn't do the deed. It also seemed improbable that he had someone else do it for him. He inherited tens of millions of dollars from his father's estate. His mother was living off of a trust that he would inherit after her death, but it only amounted to a few million more, which, in the context of his wealth, wasn't enough to provide a motive. On top of that, he and his mother appeared to have had a strong relationship. He didn't seem like a viable suspect.

And as for gold diggers, there didn't seem to be any. Governor Thompson had been dead for almost twenty years and during that time, Mrs. Thompson had had a few relationships that Agent Ready was able to find out about. But the men, including the one she had been seeing at the time of her death, were all well established in their own right, most wealthier than she'd been. Money didn't seem to be a likely motive.

So Ready was left with either a robbery gone bad or some sort of politically motivated killing. The robbery gone bad scenario didn't ring true to Agent Ready. Clearly someone had staked out her house from the spot in the woods in the back a number of times. In doing that, he would have seen that she was a creature of habit and that she swam almost every afternoon, an activity that took her away from the house for at least ninety minutes. And the cleaning lady worked mornings and the gardener and his staff worked on Tuesdays and Fridays, and they were usually done by noon.

If someone cased the place with the intent of robbing it, it would have been pretty easy to establish that the time to do it was in the late afternoon, right after she left for her swim. The killer did spend a fair amount of time watching Mrs. Thompson's house, but it didn't seem likely that he did so with the intention of robbing her.

And there was one other really strange thing. In the thorough search of the wooded area, near the spot behind the bushes where the killer had allegedly watched, agents found a cigarette butt. The butt had clear fingerprints and those prints belonged to the Mayor of Summerset. The mayor, who had been in office for fifteen years, claimed to have never set foot in those woods and had a clear alibi on the day of the murder. To make matters worse, someone had tipped of the press about the cigarette butt, something only a handful of agents and, eventually, the mayor himself knew about. That created speculation that reached the network news reports. While Ready didn't think the seventy-two year old mayor was a likely suspect, he could not understand the presence of his cigarette in the woods. One thing seemed certain, with all of the speculation going on in the press and on the news stations, the mayor's chances of winning yet another election were slim.

Chapter 14

So far, he had killed in Connecticut, Pennsylvania, Illinois and Georgia. It was time to head west. The longest-serving senator or congressman in the western half of the country was Senator David Kahele of Hawaii. He was an admirable man, awarded the Distinguished Service Cross in World War II. Murdering a relative of his would make a strong point, but Hawaii itself posed too many problems. He wanted to stay in the lower forty-eight. Maybe Kahele had a relative on the mainland.

Montana's senior senator, Rex Smithers, was another good candidate and it was time for another Democrat. He would have to do some research.

His preferred method of research was the internet. But that could be problematic because it could lead to traces. Fortunately, with regard to long-serving national politicians, there was no shortage of printed material. He could go into almost any library and find biographical information. He scanned the printed information for names of relatives and used those names as the starting point for his internet search. In that way, even if the authorities became aware of his plan, they would have to monitor searches for a lot more than 535 people. His purpose was as well served by killing a distant relative as it was a spouse or child, so he had a wide population from which to choose. But he knew that with time, researching even distant relatives would become risky, so now, while he was still anonymous, he would try to come up with five to ten names for each of about twenty senators or congressmen, or congresswomen for that matter. His point knew no party, no race and no gender.

Once he'd found a name, he'd go to a low-tech internet café, one without cameras, wearing a mild disguise. He tried to look like an average, overweight, middle-aged American male, to be as normal-looking and unremarkable as he could. He often wore a fat suit that added about forty pounds to his frame. With the suit, a wig and some sort of facial hair, different types of glasses, hats and nondescript clothes, he could dramatically change his appearance. After he was adequately disguised, he'd go to pre-screened internet cafes and rent a computer for a few hours, paying with cash. If the computer had its own camera, he covered the lens with tape. Then he consulted his list of relatives' names and, using free and paid websites like Ancestry.com and Genealogy.com, he traced their lineages. If the lineage services charged fees, he paid with anonymous prepaid credit cards that he purchased with cash at neighborhood drugstores or supermarkets. Once he actually started his internet search, he would try to find somewhat distant relatives, cousins or nephews or nieces. Occasionally he would pick higher profile relations, like Mrs. Thompson, but he wanted to try to make at least six or seven different statements before sharing his plan with the general public. To do that, he had to keep a low profile. But, he also wanted to make it clear that no one was off limits. So a mother, Mrs. Thompson, was a necessary risk. He also wanted a spouse and, most importantly, a child. But he had to be careful. For now, the statements weren't too difficult, but that would all change.

He tried not to form any opinions as he worked. He simply gathered as much information and as many potential names and addresses as he could. Then he went to a big city library and looked through phone books to confirm or update addresses for the names on his list.

Eventually, he would go back to his hotel or motel, usually something along the lines of a Best Western or Days Inn and, in the privacy of his room, go online and investigate the addresses.

He always did everything he possibly could to leave the smallest electronic trace of his actions. For example, to research the niece of Senator Smithers of Montana, who lived in Sun Prairie, just west of Great Falls, he would simply Google "Montana" or maybe even "California". Then he would select the Google Map picture that appeared and drag it and zoom in until he could find Sun Prairie. He would select the satellite view and zoom in on the specific address. He could tell and screen so much just by looking at a satellite image. In suburban or rural areas, if a property was in the middle of a subdivision with little in the way of woods or undeveloped land to provide potential cover while he did his on or near-site evaluation, the risk of discovery would be too great and the candidate would be eliminated, or actually not eliminated, but rather saved. Senator Smithers' niece was saved for several reasons. Sun Prairie was too small. A stranger hanging around there for a few days would be remembered. On top of that, her house was in the middle of a moderately sized subdivision with small lots. He preferred perimeter lots. Watching her would be difficult and killing her at home without someone at least seeing him coming or going would be next to impossible. She was safe.

So he would go over each name on the list for each politician and then come up with two or three good possibilities. Then he would travel again. He didn't really live anywhere anymore. He moved from motel to motel. When he wasn't fleeing a scene, he generally traveled by train, bus or car. It took longer, but saved money and put him under less official scrutiny than flying.

Senator Smithers' daughter, Anna, was a student at the University of Montana in Missoula. She was a promising prospect on paper, but could be an emotionally difficult kill. He also had a cousin in Billings. Both looked like strong candidates.

Chapter 15

Four weeks had passed since Mrs. Thompson's murder. Neither Chief Mountain of the Summerset Police nor Agent Ready had any idea who killed her. The mayor's name was still in the public conversation, because of the cigarette, but the authorities knew he was not a viable suspect.

Chapter 16

Greg spent hours trying to come up with a reason to call Sarah Jennings, but each idea was worse than its predecessors. Then about two weeks after he delivered the couch, he looked up from his desk and there she was.

He had the presence of mind to stand, but once again, he was speechless.

Again she led. "Hi."

And again he stumbled. God she was pretty. Finally he came back with, "Hi."

They smiled at each other. Then he realized that she had taken the time to find his address and drive the twenty or thirty minutes to find him. "Is something wrong with the couch?"

"The couch? No. It's fine." She saw the look of disappointment on his face when she said "fine" and upped her assessment, smiling. "It's great. We love it."

"Good. I'm glad." He paused. "How's your mother?"

"She's fine. Thanks."

"Good. I'm glad." He blushed, realizing he had just said that. "What, um, do you need something else reupholstered?"

She laughed again, at him, but in a nice way. "I thought you would call me."

"You did?" They looked into each other's eyes and exchanged an understanding. There was something there. "I wanted to call you. I have been trying to think of excuses to … reasons to. You know, reasons that would make sense."

She smiled. "Do you want to have lunch?"

"Today?"

"Yes. Now."

"Yes."

Chapter 17

Senator Smithers' daughter Anna turned out to be a very promising target. She lived in a dorm that was near the university's recreation center, the stadium, and one of the largest student cafeterias. The dorm abutted a large, crowded parking lot and there was a ton of activity in the area. He could easily blend in and watch her for a few days without drawing any attention. However, killing her in such a busy area would be difficult. He couldn't risk going into her dorm or trying to kill her on campus. Even at night, there was too much activity. He needed to kill at least four more people before he took that sort of risk.

After two days, he thought he might have to give up on her. She never seemed to be alone or to leave the campus or the nearby town. She was a nice looking girl, not gorgeous, but pretty and fit and happy. He liked watching her, liked her smile. How did she stay so fit? He hadn't seen her work out yet. He parked in the big lot near her dorm each morning at about 8 and watched her throughout the day and well into the evening. She went to class, to meals, to the library, but he hadn't seen her go to the Rec Center or anywhere else to work out.

The next morning, he decided to go to the campus at 6. He parked in a spot that was a fair way from her dorm, but at the edge of the lot, giving him an unobstructed view of the building's main entrance. He sat wearing old gray sweatpants, a navy blue hooded sweatshirt, sunglasses and a baseball cap, pretending to read the paper he was holding. If anyone questioned him about what he was doing, he would say he was going to go for a run, but that he was waiting for someone. He would sit reading for a while longer and then appear to give up on the person he was waiting for and go for a run on his own. After the run, he would leave Missoula and leave the senator's daughter untouched.

But no one questioned him.

At 6:30, she came out of the dorm. She was wearing running clothes. He put down his paper and got out of the car. He stood beside the car and started to stretch.

She zipped up her jacket, retied her shoes and started to run towards him, along the sidewalk in front of her dorm. As he ran past, she noticed he was in running clothes too and gave him a friendly smile.

He smiled back and waited, continuing to stretch. He willed himself to wait longer. After about ninety seconds, he shook out his legs and began a slow jog after her, about three or four hundred yards behind. She was running along a main sidewalk that ran between the cafeteria and the stadium. There weren't many people out at that early hour. He would have to stay well behind her not to freak her out, and even then only for a short distance. Past the stadium, the main sidewalk branched off in several directions, two into the campus and one to the campus perimeter. He would have to go in a different direction once she made her choice.

She reached the junction and turned to the right, following the sidewalk to the edge of the campus. He slowed his pace, staying well behind and watching her, maximizing the time before he got to the junction. She crossed the road that marked the edge of the campus and followed what appeared to be a trail into a heavily wooded area of undeveloped, hilly land.

He watched as she disappeared into the trees. When he got to the junction where she'd gone to the right, he went left, into the main part of the campus. He decided he would go for a short run, just over a mile and then pretend to tire and slow to a walk as he came back within view of her dorm. Hopefully she would run for longer than that so he could see her return and get a sense of her routine.

Ten minutes later, he slowed and walked back to his car. There was no sign of her. He sat inside the car and drank a bottle of water and waited. About twenty-five minutes later, she came into view, still running. She ran by without noticing him and stopped as she reached her dorm.

He went back to his room at the Motel 6 and waited for a few hours, reading papers and watching the news. There was no mention of Mrs. Thompson.

At noon, he drove back to the university, this time wearing longish black running shorts, a gray sweatshirt and an old white Dallas Cowboys baseball cap. He parked in a different lot, near the northeast corner of the campus. He casually walked along a perimeter sidewalk to the trail Anna took that morning.

At its entrance, the trail was wide and well maintained. He entered the path and started to jog slowly along, following the only direction it offered. The trail wandered but generally moved east, away from the campus. After about a mile, it split. The right branch went up hill and the left one went down. Most runners choose to take hills early in a run rather than later, so he turned right and kept running. Anna's run had lasted about forty minutes and he thought she was running at about an eight minute per mile pace, so he figured she had run about five miles. He estimated that he had run about two when the hill crested and the trail veered to the left, north, along the hill's ridgeline. There were a few smaller trails going out from the main trail, but none seemed like good running spots, especially for a girl by herself running at Anna's pace.

In another mile, there was another fork in the trail. One path led to the left, back in the general direction of the campus to the west and the other continued north, along the top of the ridge. He was about three miles into the run. If Anna did come this way, to be back in the time she was, it was most likely that she cut back in here. But he decided to keep going straight along the ridge for another mile or so, to see if there was another route back towards the campus that she could have taken. Eventually there was, about two miles further on, but it was too far for her to have gone and made it back to the campus in the time she had. He turned around and ran back along the ridge until he came to the path, on his right now, that led back down the hill, towards the school. He followed it and, sure enough, it led back to the original path he had followed from the campus's edge. She would have almost certainly run the same circular course. He might not have the direction she ran right, but if she ran here every morning, this was her route. He walked back over the trail, looking for his spot.

Chapter 18

The idea that the murders were somehow connected bothered Chief Mason. He went online and googled the words "murder" and "Congress". He got 110 million results. He refined his search adding the word "relative" and "2013" and "2014". That slimmed his options down to a mere 38 million results. He started reading. Both Mrs. Thompson and Mr. Boeckh appeared frequently in the first several pages of search results as did Gabby Gifford and the Kennedys. He skimmed through a number of older cases until he came across the name John Carroll. Carroll was an African American from a southwestern suburb of Chicago, Mayfield. He had been murdered in his home on April 14, 2014. He was a cousin of Representative Michael Simpson, a congressman from Chicago's South Side. Simpson, who was in his sixteenth term in the US House of Representatives, was quoted saying that he was sorry to hear of his distant relative's death, but that he had only met him once or twice, at family weddings or funerals. Carroll was bludgeoned with a hammer, his own hammer. It didn't appear that police had made any progress in finding the murderer.

Chief Mason wrote down the name of the town, Mayfield, and then googled "John Carroll", "Mayfield" and "Congress". He read several newspaper articles on the murder and jotted down the name of the Mayfield police chief, Pete Hunsinger.

He tracked down the number of the Mayfield PD and called Chief Hunsinger. At first, Hunsinger was reluctant to discuss the case because he was both unsure of Mason's credentials and curious about the reasons for his interest.

Mason gave him his number and asked that Chief Hunsinger call Information to verify the number for the Harrison PD and then call the department himself. Hunsinger did and asked for the Chief. Mason answered.

The two discussed the case for about thirty minutes. Aside from the murder weapon, Hunsinger didn't have much. In the woods near Mr. Carroll's home, officers found evidence of a stakeout, including a discarded McDonald's coffee cup. They found fingerprints on the cup, but the prints led the police on a wild goose chase. They belonged to the mayor of Winnetka, an affluent town north of Chicago. Hunsinger and his department spent a great deal of time checking into the mayor's background. He had been in office for over twenty years and was clean as a whistle. And he had been in Wisconsin on the day of the murder. Neither he nor the police department could figure out how a coffee cup with his fingerprints ended up in Mayfield.

Chapter 19

For the next two years, Greg and Sarah spent as much time as they could together. She lived off campus in an apartment with two other girls at Fordham. By her senior year, Greg was spending most of his nights there.

While Mrs. Jennings liked Greg and was sympathetic to his situation, at first she quietly opposed their dating. She and her husband, who left her when Sarah was a young child, were both teachers, and she put a great deal of value on the importance of a college education. So, while she did like Greg and understood why he had to leave college and was even impressed by his actions, she wanted more for her daughter. But she eventually realized there wasn't anything she could do about it and that her daughter loved him. So she put her reservations aside and embraced him. Sarah was all she had and she wanted her to be happy and didn't want to lose her.

Greg's mom, Janet, liked Sarah from the start. She felt bad for her son. He had given up his own education and dreams to support her and his sisters. And both sisters were in college now. While her husband's life insurance policy was helping to pay for their educations, Greg earned the money that fed them and kept the roof over their heads. Now that the girls were older and more independent, Janet was working full time at the shop, handling the retail clients and slowly taking on the responsibilities of their aging bookkeeper, but it was Greg who made the business prosper.

Janet was glad he'd found Sarah. He had done a great job with the upholstery business and she wanted him to have a life of his own, away from work.

The summer Sarah graduated, they married. They rented an apartment in Garden City and Sarah got a job teaching second grade at MacArthur Elementary.

Chapter 20

The next morning, he parked at the far end of the parking lot near her dorm, by the back of the stadium. From his spot, he could see both the entry to her dorm and the head of the running trail leading into the woods.

At 6:33, she came out and started running. He watched her gait lengthen as her muscles loosened. By the time she disappeared behind the stadium, she was almost to full stride. Then he waited, hoping she would run the same route again, instead of varying it and staying on campus. He looked at his watch as she ran out of sight, 6:36. He figured that if she was going to run on the trail again, he would see her come out from behind the stadium in about two minutes.

This would be the hardest statement for him. She was young and seemingly kind and innocent. He hadn't liked killing any of them, not even the old drunk in Pennsylvania. None of them deserved to die.

There she was. She came to the road at the edge of the campus, looked both ways without breaking stride, and then crossed the street and disappeared onto the trail into woods.

A little over forty minutes later, she was back.

He waited fifteen more minutes then drove back to his hotel.

Chapter 21

Mason couldn't believe what he'd stumbled upon. Was there someone out there deliberately killing relatives of US senators and congressmen? Was he the only one who had figured it out?

He went over the three killings again and again, gathering as much evidence as he could and trying to find connections. There were several. First, all three victims were related to sitting members of Congress. Second, there was very little in the way of evidence at any of the three crime scenes, at least so far as Chief Mason could tell. He knew that police often withheld key pieces of evidence to help solve crimes. He had used the same tactic to try to solve a murder in his own town. While the tactic eventually worked and helped him find the killer, it had taken years and had not saved an innocent man's life.

He looked back down at his notes. Third, the victims had all been alone and there was evidence that they had been watched. And fourth, in two cases apparently false evidence was left behind, evidence that attempted to implicate local politicians.

Fifth, did he have a fifth?

He looked through his notes and the Google stories he had printed out, scanning the headlines. Illinois, Pennsylvania, then Connecticut. Was he moving east? Would he go to Washington next? Was there a geographic pattern? East to west? So what.

Was there a motive? If he was right that these people were killed not because of who they were or what they had done, but because of whom they were related to, then there had to be some connection between the three elected officials.

He googled the politicians names together. "Thompson", "Boeckh" and "Carroll". 385,000 results. He scanned the early articles. Nothing he found really linked the three. One was a Democrat and two were Republicans. The three hadn't co-sponsored any bills that he could find.

They were all pretty old. He checked their ages. Two of the three were quite old. Boeckh was the longest-serving congressman in the state's history. Thompson wasn't Connecticut's longest-serving senator ever, but he was in his fourth term. And Simpson? He checked his notes. Nothing. He googled him. He was in his eighteenth term, his thirty-fifth year in Congress. Could that be the link? Was this guy indirectly going after long-serving congressmen and senators?

He thought about it. Congressional approval ratings were as low as they had ever been. Ninety percent of the country thought they were doing a bad job. He laughed to himself, thinking that's a lot of potential suspects.

Chapter 22

Greg and Sarah easily settled in together. She finished work a couple of hours before he did, so she would come home, do chores, work out and, if they were going to eat at home that night, make dinner. She got to know several other young teachers from her school and between those women and friends she and Greg knew from growing up in the area, they developed a pretty active social life. But mostly they just enjoyed each other.

Greg loved to fish and he owned a small boat that had been his father's. After his dad died, he thought about selling it, but because it was old and beat up it wasn't worth much, so he decided to keep it. The boat was a 19 foot, center console Grady-White. His dad had been the third owner and the first two hadn't taken very good care of it. But it ran and got him out on the Long Island Sound when he wanted to get away. It had been his refuge in the early days after his dad died, but now, since he had been married, he hardly used it at all.

One day, Sarah asked him to take her out fishing. He was surprised but pleased by her suggestion. He hooked the boat and trailer to the back of his van and drove to the Port Jefferson public landing.

Greg told Sarah he was glad she hadn't been with him the first time he'd tried to back the trailer down the ramp. He explained that it is difficult because when you back up a trailer the steering is counterintuitive. On top of that, the landing at Port Jeff is very narrow and there's always a group of old-timers standing around, making rookies feel inept. The first time he did it, he'd been totally humiliated. It had been a busy Saturday morning and it took him three or four tries before he successfully backed down the ramp.

She surprised him by asking if she could give it a try.

"It's really hard Sarah, and it's a beautiful Saturday morning, the place is going to be a zoo."

"So? Who cares?"

He laughed as he drove into the parking area by the landing. There was already a line of five SUVs with trailers. Greg pulled into the line and turned to face his wife. "You sure you want to try? It's really crowded today."

She leaned over and unfastened his seatbelt. "Get out."

He laughed again. "Okay. Don't say I didn't warn you."

They opened their doors and got out, switching sides. Greg watched as a couple of the locals pointed at the babe getting into the driver's side. He could only imagine what they were saying about her – and about him for that matter. He watched her as she watched the drivers in line ahead of her pull up to the wide space in front of the landing and then turn away from it and back in. Some made it look so simple and others struggled.

She didn't say a word.

"Do you have any questions?"

She looked at him and smiled. "Nope."

He smiled too.

When their turn came, he felt his anxiety rise. "You sure you want to do this? Really, it's a lot harder than it looks."

"I've got it, Greg. But do me a favor, stand over there, by the tight side and let me know if I am getting too close."

He opened his door and got out of the car, uncertain whether she really wanted his help or was just getting him out of her hair. He stood by an unfortunately placed block of embedded concrete that limited the driver's range in the blind spot over his or her right shoulder.

Once he was in place, with about a dozen men and several women watching closely, Sarah pulled past the landing and cut the wheel to the left, then pulled away from the water. Greg watched. So far so good. He wanted to coach her, but felt his comments from outside would only complicate matters, so he kept quiet. The van's reverse lights came on. She started back. At first, it appeared as though she might be cutting too much, that she might bring the back of the boat and trailer right into the concrete, but she seemed to realize her error and corrected. On her first try, she backed the trailer in, right down the middle of the ramp. As she finished backing the boat and trailer into the water, he caught her eyes in the van's passenger side rearview mirror. She flashed him a gorgeous smile.

Chapter 23

The next morning, he left his hotel room at 5:15 wearing gray sweats, a faded dark brown hoody, a blue baseball cap and a lightweight nylon runner's pack. He had the hood up, over the hat. Under the hat he wore a black, shaggy looking wig.

He drove to a quiet wooded street of off-campus student housing about a mile or so from the trailhead and parked. Then he leaned over, as if picking up something from the passenger side floor and patted a baseball player style Fu Manchu mustache and beard into place. He sat up and secured it as he looked in the mirror, appearing to any onlooker as if he was simply stroking and smoothing out his scruffy facial hair. Confident that it was securely in place, he put on his sunglasses and got out of the car. Then he started to run, lumbering as if it was a struggle. In ten minutes, he was at the trailhead. He increased his pace and hurried to his spot.

Chapter 24

At 6:15, Anna woke up. It was Friday. She had been out late the night before, but she wanted to get her run in. Her roommate rolled over in her bed, moaning at Anna's movements. The senator's daughter looked out the window. The sky was gray, again. She slipped off her pajamas and put on her running clothes then went to the bathroom and brushed her teeth.

By 6:30, she was outside and started running. As usual, unless there was rain or snow, she decided to run on the trail to the east of the campus. She loved running there.

In spite of her late night, Anna's legs felt light and strong. She could never tell whether she was going to have a good run or a bad one until she started. This was going to be a good one. When she hit the trail she looked at her watch and picked up her speed. She felt great.

About a mile into the trail, she came to the fork. Usually if she felt strong, she went the to the right, choosing the immediate steep climb over the easier gradual climb to the left. Today she felt as though she could break her personal record. She powered up the hill, reaching the ridge and heading north. Her stride increased. In another mile, she approached the next fork. Sometimes when she felt really good, she would stay on the ridge and turn her five-mile run into an eight-miler. She considered it, but knew she needed to do a little work before her nine o'clock economics class. She cut left and started to fly down the gradual hill.

Chapter 25

He waited. If she was running the steep route first, he was in the perfect position. If she was coming from the gradual side, his task would be more difficult. And that was if she was even running today. For all he knew, she was still in bed.

The spot he picked was perfect. It was on one the steepest portions of this side of the trail. From what he hoped would be her perspective, running down the hill, the trail turned to the left and dropped off sharply around a massive rock outcropping. He was behind the outcropping, hidden from the uphill view. He'd taken a black disposable jumpsuit from his pack and was wearing it and a pair of surgical gloves.

He heard the sound of a runner in the distance, of shoes hitting dirt.

Whoever was coming was coming fast.

He'd tied a length of wire to a tree on the other side of the trail, about twelve feet from where he crouched, then wrapped his end around the trunk of a small tree on his side. The wire was slack, but when yanked taut, it snapped to about ten inches above the ground.

The runner was close now. He looked behind the rock outcropping, up the hill. It was the senator's daughter. Using the tree near him to absorb most of the expected impact and to save his hands, he pulled the wire tight. Seconds later, her left foot came into view. The wire tugged. He held it fast. Her stride changed. Her front foot came to an abrupt stop and the back foot's tip caught the wire. Her lower body stopped but her upper body kept going, surging forward, tumbling face first to the trail.

Chapter 26

She was flying, effortlessly. She felt so good. Her eyes caught a glimmer of movement at her feet but it was too late. Something cut into her left shin and caught the toe of her right shoe. Her feet stopped as her upper body lunged forward. She saw more movement. A man. She put out her hand to brace her fall. Her left arm was already up and bore the brunt of the impact. But her momentum kept her rolling forward, ass-over-head, into the dirt and roots and rocks. She had to get up, to keep moving. She sensed him getting up and coming towards her. She kept going, trying to roll to her feet. Just as she was about to get back up, he was on her. She rammed her elbow back at him, catching his torso. He grunted, but his momentum kept him going too. His left arm came around her, then his right. Her panic increased when she saw he was wearing surgical gloves. He joined his hands and held her then suddenly and forcefully yanked them back. Her forward momentum stopped. She felt something cutting into her neck, wire. She struggled, kicking and elbowing him, trying to reach back and scratch his face. He tightened the wire and moved his face away, dodging each desperate lash of her fingers and nails. She couldn't make him stop.

Chapter 27

All night, all week, he'd dreaded this murder. He wasn't sure if he could do it. She was too young.

But it all happened so quickly that he didn't have time to think. She was strong and fast. She tried to stop him and fought hard, but he was behind her and bigger and stronger and she was losing her air. He pulled tight. She started to weaken. The force of her kicks and elbows lessened, but her efforts continued. She was amazing. He held tight. Her legs seemed to give way and she collapsed back into him. He collapsed into the trail and held on to the wire, feeling her against him, her back to his chest. He could feel her chest heaving, trying to get air. Then it stopped. He felt her die. For a minute, maybe more, he just sat there. Holding the wire, feeling her body against his.

What had he done? What was he doing?

He stood, gently easing her body to the ground. He didn't want to look at her.

His first instinct was to simply leave, but he needed to create more time before her body was found. He bent and slipped one arm under her shoulders and the other under her knees. He lifted her and carried her back up the hill to the outcropping and then into the woods, about two hundred feet from the trail. He didn't dare to look at her face. He stepped over a fallen pine tree and carefully placed her against the wide trunk, on the side away from the trail. He covered her with sticks and leaves.

He snapped a dried out branch from the dead pine and made his way back to the trail, using the branch to brush sticks and leaves over the trail of his footsteps. When he looked back to the fallen tree from the trail, he couldn't see her or any obvious evidence of his tracks. He collected both the wire he'd used to strangle her and the longer one he tripped her with and put them into a baggie and then into his nylon daypack. Then he removed his black disposable jumpsuit and put it in the pack. There would be tracks from his shoes that might eventually be found, but he was wearing the best selling brand of Nike running shoes – the Supernovas – in a twelve, with two pairs of thick socks. While he had muddied them up so that they wouldn't look new, this was only the second time he had worn them. The tracks from the soles wouldn't yet reveal anything much about his particular stride.

He double-checked the scene and then headed back up the trail, to the ridge. Once he reached the top and came to the merger with the ongoing trail, he turned left and north, running along the ridge, taking the longer route that Anna had fatefully decided to forego. He ran the extra two miles and then followed the trail down to the road, at the northeast corner of the campus, not far from where he'd parked.

Chapter 28

Mason decided it was time. He called the FBI and asked for the agent in charge of the Thompson case, Sean Ready.

The agent who took the call said that Agent Ready wasn't available and that he would take any information the caller wanted to pass along. But Mason wanted to talk to Ready himself. He told the agent that he was the chief of police in Harrison, Pennsylvania and that he thought he might have some information pertaining to the Thompson murder.

Forty minutes later, Ready called back.

"Chief Mason?"

"Yes?"

"This is Agent Ready, from the FBI, returning your call."

"Thanks for calling me back."

"No problem. My colleague said that you have some information about the Thompson case?"

"I said I might have some information…"

Ready cut him off. "Look Chief, um Mason. If you have something just tell me what it is."

Mason took a breath and then started. "Agent Ready, I think that Mrs. Thompson's murder may be related to a murder that took place here in Pennsylvania and to another in suburban Chicago." He paused, to gauge the agent's reaction.

Ready gave nothing away. If he knew of the other two murders, he didn't admit it. Acknowledging the chief's pause he said, "Go on. You've got my attention."

Mason started again. "I'm not sure I'm right about all of this Agent Ready, but there are just too many links. I figured, I should bring it to your attention."

Ready could hear the sincerity in the policeman's voice and decided to give him a real listen. "Go ahead, Chief Mason. Let me hear what you've got."

"Okay. Well, as you know, Mrs. Thompson is Senator Thompson's mother."

He heard Ready breathe into the phone. "Well, the brother of Congressman John Boeckh, an elderly man named Doug Boeckh, was murdered here in Pennsylvania on March 11th, 2014. He was stabbed in the ear."

He paused to let that sink in, but wanted to get the next murder out before the agent had a chance to comment. "And on April 14th of this year, a man named John Carroll was murdered in Mayfield, Illinois. Mr. Carroll is the cousin of Congressman Michael Simpson, from Chicago."

Ready listened, letting the chief go on.

"The murders all have several things in common, Agent Ready."

Ready was recording the conversation, but now he was also taking notes. "Go ahead, Chief. Lay it all out."

Mason could hear the increased interest in the agent's voice. "Okay. First, as I said, all three victims are related to a sitting congressman or a senator. Second, in all three murders, there was very little if any evidence left behind. But the murder weapons were, and they were all possessions of the victims: a knife for Mrs. Thompson, a letter opener for Mr. Boeckh, actually a congressional letter opener that his brother had given him, and a hammer for Mr. Carroll. The murders all appear to have been done by someone who had thought it through and had time to find murder weapons in the victims' houses. Third, there's evidence that all three victims had been watched. The other two cases are like the one you've been looking into, Mrs. Thompson's."

The chief paused, he wasn't sure if Ready had already made the connections he had, whether he already knew about the other two.

Ready was silent so Mason went on. "In two of the three cases, Mrs. Thompson's and Mr. Carroll's, there was seemingly false evidence left at the scene. The cigarette butt in the woods by Mrs. Thompson's house implicating the Mayor of Summerset, and a paper coffee cup was found in the woods near Mr. Carroll's house. The cup had the prints of the Mayor of Winnetka, Illinois, which is a suburb north of Chicago."

"Next, all three politicians have been in Congress for a long time. Boeckh is the longest-serving congressman or senator in the history of Pennsylvania, 39 years. Simpson is in his 17th term and his 35th year and your guy, Senator Thompson, is in his fourth term in the Senate. He's in his 22nd year in office, and he served two terms as a congressman before that."

He paused, letting that sink in.

Ready filled the gap. "Anything else?"

Mason couldn't tell whether the question was sarcastic or sincere. Cautiously he replied, "Just one more common thing. The two politicians who were set up or framed, they were both long-serving too. Both over ten years as mayor."

Ready couldn't believe what he was hearing. These were strong connections and while they could be unrelated, he doubted it.

"How did you figure this all out, Chief?"

"Well, on the night of Mrs. Thompson's murder, I was watching the news and saw the interviews you and the Summerset police chief gave and it made me think of the murder in my state, the murder of Mr. Boeckh. I did some research on it and that made me wonder if there might be any others, so I started looking and came up with Mr. Carroll. Carroll is admittedly a more distant relative, a second cousin, than Mrs. Thompson as the mother, obviously, or Mr. Boeckh as a brother, but, given that false evidence was left behind there, the coffee cup, implicating a long-serving mayor in a nearby town, well I think there is a pretty clear link to the Thompson murder."

Ready couldn't disagree, but he didn't say anything.

"Where did you get all of this information, Chief?"

"Mostly online and I talked with the Chief of the Jefferson PD, where Mr. Boeckh lived and the Chief of the Mayfield PD, where Mr. Carroll lived. But I got most of it by googling."

Ready was astounded and a little embarrassed. He was a good enough guy to give the chief some credit.

"Listen Chief Mason, I really appreciate you calling me. You have certainly given us a lot to look into. I'm not saying that you have found a link here, but you were certainly right in bringing this to our attention."

He paused on those words. Mason knew what his next question would be. He saved him the time.

"I haven't told anyone else about this, Agent Ready, not even the other two police chiefs. For one thing, I don't know if it's right. I think there are too many coincidences for there not to be something to this. The last thing I wanted to do was to bother you with a bunch of junk. And also, I appreciate how sensitive this information is. If I am right, I don't want to be the one breaking this story, Agent Ready. The media is going to go nuts with this. Better you than me."

Ready was starting to like this guy.

"Okay, Chief. I appreciate you calling and I appreciate you keeping all of this to yourself. In light of what you just said, I don't think I need to say this, but I will anyway. I would appreciate it if you didn't tell anyone else about this, if you continue to keep it to yourself. Let us look into all of this and see what we can put together and, if it is necessary, we'll figure how to let the news out."

"I understand. Like I said, better you than me."

Ready thought for a minute and then asked, "So you've been thinking about this since you heard about Mrs. Thompson's murder, the night she was killed?"

Mason wasn't too sure about the motive behind the question and he answered cautiously. "Yes, it did occur to me the first night, but I didn't really put it all together until yesterday, and even after I did, I wanted to sleep on it for a night before I bothered you guys. I wanted to be sure I had something worth bothering you with."

"I understand and heck, you found this." He didn't add what he was thinking: before we did. "The reason for my question is, what did you think that first night, or more importantly, what do you think you have here, Chief?"

Mason hadn't said it to anyone out loud. He paused and then

said, "I think that maybe there is some crazy guy out there who is systematically killing relatives of members of the US Congress, long-serving ones. The guy obviously has a huge grudge against the government. I haven't been sure what to make of the long-serving aspect. Maybe his gripe is about something that happened a long time ago, or maybe he thinks that if the government is bad, then someone who has been with the government for a long time is especially bad."

Chapter 29

He paid for his hotel room through the next day and left the "Do not disturb" tab on the door handle and the TV on in his room. He didn't return after the murder. He had already wiped down the room and removed the few belongings he brought inside with him. As a rule, he didn't bring much into his hotel rooms: generally just a good-sized daypack that carried one change of clothing, his toiletries and his laptop. If he needed more things in the room, he would bring them in and take them out separately. That way when he was on the road, he could always leave without needing to go back to the hotel and without leaving much of a trace.

After he finished his "run", he had simply gotten back in his car and headed south, disposing of the things he'd used in the murder in much the same way he had in the past, piecemeal, hundreds of miles from the crime scene and in seemingly innocent, separate drops.

Fifteen hours after the murder, he was at a Days Inn in Colorado Springs. He decided to stay there for a few days and then head to his next statement destination. In the meantime, he intended to spend a lot of time watching the news, on television and online. He suspected that once Anna's body was found, the death of a second senator's relative would lead the authorities and the media into frenzies. He had been waiting for this for a long time. He checked his list. He had fifteen potential victims he could stakeout without needing to go back online. That stage of his advance work was already done.

Chapter 30

About two years after they were married, on a warm, sunny Sunday afternoon on Memorial Day weekend, Greg was in the yard, painting an old picnic table. Midway through the painting, he decided to do some repairs to the table and as a result, it turned into quite a messy job. His hands were covered in white paint and there were splatters on his face and in his hair.

Sarah called down to him. "Greg. I need you up here."

Even though she was about nine months pregnant, he wasn't especially responsive when she called because rather than going for a long run, as he had planned, he was doing a bunch of chores she wanted him to do before the baby came, chores that he'd been putting off for some time. The table was somewhere around number six on that day's list and he didn't know how many more items there were. So he moaned inwardly and responded, "Sarah, I'm painting the picnic table. Can it wait?"

"No. I don't think so."

He muttered to himself and crawled out from under the table. "What is it?" As he asked, he looked up to her. She was standing about fifteen feet above him on the deck that overlooked their backyard.

"I think it's time."

He couldn't really see her. The sun was almost directly behind her and her face and body were silhouetted.

"Time for what?"

"The baby. I think I'm in labor."

From that moment, things were a blur. He ran upstairs, quickly tried to wash the paint from his hands and face and then grabbed her hospital bag, his wallet and the keys. He helped her down the steep steps from the deck to the yard and around to the driveway. She had a contraction and winced. At this point, they were both at least outwardly calm.

As they approached the car, their brand new Jeep Cherokee, he started to lead her to the passenger side front seat.

"Back seat. Your side."

Her voice was strained but uncharacteristically authoritative. He opened the rear driver side door and helped her in. The car was facing in and their driveway was tight, especially because of the wet, half white picnic table to Greg's left, so he backed cautiously out onto their busy street.

They were at the age when lots of their friends were having babies and had heard horror stories of fifteen and twenty hour labors. Greg wished he'd eaten lunch.

The hospital that Sarah's doctor used was several towns away, in Rosedale. As Greg pulled onto the Long Island Expressway, she had another contraction, a seemingly more painful one.

"How far apart was that from the last one?"

Sarah didn't answer at first. She was still riding a wave of pain. He looked at her in the rearview mirror and saw her face. For the first time that day, he was scared.

Thankfully there wasn't much traffic. He was going about 75 in a 55 miles per hour zone, hurrying, but not frantic.

"I'm not sure, not very long."

He weaved through the traffic, watching her and the road ahead.

She cried out again. It couldn't have been much more than a minute later. "Holy shit. Was that another contraction or the same one?"

Again she didn't answer. She was standing in front of the back seat, her hands on each of the front seats' headrests, her nails digging into the vinyl.

He tried to watch her and drive as she rode through the contraction, feeling totally helpless. He increased his speed.

"I don't know. They're coming so fast."

He was stuck behind some old guy in a hat, going about ten in the left hand lane. The center lane was blocked too. He pounded the horn and the old guy seemed to slow even more.

He looked two lanes to the right and saw an opening and took it, slowing to get some space, then cutting right and accelerating. He expected her to tell him to be careful, but she didn't even notice. Once he was past the two slow cars, he had open road and accelerated back into the left hand lane. He was going about 90 now. If a cop came, he would gratefully pay any fine.

He sensed movement in the backseats and looked back over his shoulder.

His wife was undressing.

"What are you doing?"

She was wearing a one-piece maternity pantsuit and had the top half pulled down to her waist.

"I'm taking my clothes off." She didn't add, "You idiot."

"Why?" His voice was unsure.

"Because I saw on Oprah that women sometimes have babies in their pants."

She was making no sense.

"What?"

She pulled the pantsuit down her legs and pulled her feet free. She was in the backseat, nine months pregnant, sort of standing-squatting, her hands on the headrests in front of her, wearing only her bra and a pair of seriously big panties.

"What are you doing, Sarah?"

"I'm going to have this baby. Any minute. I don't want to have it into my pants." She screamed again and then sat back into the seat.

Greg was approaching the Rosedale exit, where the hospital was. He moved into the right hand lane and made a sharp right, following the exit ramp. He looked over his shoulder to Sarah. She was squatting again, holding the seat backs, her legs spread. The baby's head was coming out.

He didn't really know his way around Rosedale and only knew the general area of the hospital. While Sarah had been there many times to see her doctor, Greg had only been once, for a sonogram. He headed in the hospital's general direction, up a steep hill, through the retail part of the town. He looked everywhere for a policeman, but couldn't find one.

Sarah screamed again and yelled, "Pull over, Greg."

He considered what to do. The baby was about halfway out. "No. We have to get to the hospital."

She seemed to push again and the baby came out more. He sped up the hill, going at least fifty. Where the hell were the cops? He looked back again. The baby was out, all red and wet, but out. Sarah had it in her hands and brought it to her chest.

He reached the top of the hill and a red light. He looked back at her, at them. She was seated now, holding the baby on her chest, the cord still connected. She was incredible, but looked scared.

At this moment, more than any other moment in his life, he wanted to comfort her and tell her how amazing she was. Instead, he had to do the opposite. He swallowed every scintilla of pride and asked, "Which way do I go from here?"

She looked up from the baby to him, stupefied by the question. In later years, he would claim that she responded, "Do you want me to fucking drive the car, too?" but truthfully, he wasn't sure. What did happen was that two minutes later she had directed him to the hospital and as they approached, rather than going to the emergency entrance, which was no where to been seen, he drove up to the main, front entrance. In Sarah's version of the story, Greg then leapt from the car and, for no apparent reason, opened all five doors. Finally, after consulting her, he ran inside to get help.

He sprinted to the reception desk and was greeted by an overly friendly, blue-haired, volunteer receptionist. She attempted to smile and welcome him to Rosedale Hospital.

"My wife had a baby." He pointed to the exit outside, thirty feet away. "There, in our car."

The elderly woman looked and saw an SUV, with all of its doors opened. In the back seat sat an apparently naked woman with a newborn baby on her chest.

She turned to Greg and said, "Oh my."

"Get help."

Greg ran back out to Sarah. He squatted by the door beside her. She seemed pretty calm. She was holding the baby to her, keeping it warm.

"Help is coming. They should be here soon."

He looked around. An elderly couple was sitting on a bench on the sidewalk just in front of the car, stoically watching. It was surreal. Several minutes later, there was still no help. The baby's face looked a little blue and both Greg and Sarah were getting scared. He ran back inside.

The blue-haired greeter was frantically paging through some sort of three-ringed binder.

"Where are the doctors?"

She looked up at him, fumbling through the binder. "I can't find the code for 'baby born in a car'."

Greg looked at her in disbelief. "Do you mean you haven't called for help yet?"

He didn't even wait for her response. Instead he started to yell and run up and down the front hall of the hospital, pleading for a doctor.

Kathy Connor, an off-duty nurse who was at the hospital for migraine treatments, heard a man in the hall screaming that his wife had a baby in the car and that he needed a doctor. She later said that while he seemed like a complete lunatic, there was genuine fear in his voice, so she decided to help.

Unbeknownst to the lunatic, she went out the door and found Sarah sitting alone holding a newborn to her chest in the backseat of a Jeep. She approached her and saw that the umbilical cord was still connected and that the woman was sitting on it. Rather than panicking the new mother, Kathy used a pretense to get her to shift and she pulled the cord free.

She saw that the baby was breathing and was impressed to see that Sarah had cleared her throat. The three of them were there together for a minute or two before the lunatic from inside returned. He had paint on his face and in his hair. He seemed relieved to see her there and Kathy assured him that everything would be all right. Moments later, a team of doctors and nurses and orderlies came rushing to the car.

The doctors cut the umbilical cord in the car, and left it there, and some of the team rushed the baby inside, to a sterile environment. Then they helped Sarah from the car into a wheel chair. A policeman, who had arrived on the scene, probably because someone had reported that there was a madman in the front hall, covered Sarah in newspapers. The old couple remained on the bench, simply watching.

Sarah and Greg were taken to an elevator and up to the maternity ward.

The elevator door opened into the waiting room and as it opened Sarah was greeted by silence and then cheers and applause. Apparently this room full of expectant friends and relatives of other pregnant women had seen the team of doctors and nurses come rushing up with the baby and put two and two together and realized what this new mother had done. Greg had never been so proud of her.

Minutes later, forty-five minutes after she had called him while he was under the picnic table, the two sat alone in a room.

"It's a girl."

He couldn't even respond. He beamed and kissed his incredible wife.

Chapter 31

Agent Ready couldn't believe what the small-town police chief had told him, but he knew that the man was probably on to something.

He immediately briefed his boss and the members of his team and started to look into the other two murders. Until that point, no one at the Federal Bureau of Investigation had connected the three homicides.

In the case of the Pennsylvania killling, of the congressman's brother, regional agents had made inquiries, but Jefferson police were convinced that the murder was related to gambling debts. They had decided to leave it to the locals.

And in the case of the murder in Illinois, the victim was only a distant relative. While local press reports had mentioned that the deceased, Mr. Carroll, was a distant cousin of Congressman Simpson from Chicago, the tie was so loose that it had never occurred to anyone that the murder was politically motivated.

But as soon as he started to read up on the case, Ready knew that Chief Mason was right. The Caroll murder was tied to the Thompson murder. They both were. He wondered if there were more.

Chapter 32

He decided that for his next three statements, he would pick the victims and figure out how he would kill them all before he actually did any of the killings. In that way, he would be under less pressure as he reconnoitered and, if he chose to, he could kill them in quick succession.

The potential victims were in Arizona, South Carolina and Florida. He had names and vetted addresses of two or three relatives in each state so he wouldn't need to do additional internet searches for any of them.

While he was in Colorado Springs, he purchased a black 2005 Ford Explorer with about 82,000 miles on it. He explained to the used car salesman that he had just gone through a nasty divorce and that he moved from out east to Colorado, and was going to start all over out there. He hadn't even opened a new checking account and as a result, wanted to pay in cash. He said that he had a BMW out east, but that he sold it there, before he came to Colorado Springs. Most of his assets were tied up in the divorce settlement, but he had received a cashier's check for the sale of the BMW and cashed it when he arrived in Colorado. He wanted to use what was left of that cash to pay for the Explorer.

The salesman feigned interest in the story, but he could tell he wasn't really listening.

Chapter 33

Anna's roommate Cristina got up at noon. Anna wasn't around, but that was normal. Cristina showered and went to lunch and then to her classes. She texted Anna at about three o'clock, on her way into her last class before the weekend.

When she came out at four, she checked her texts. There was no response from Anna.

She walked back to her dorm room. There was still no sign of Anna.

Then she called her and seconds later heard Anna's phone vibrating on the nightstand by her bed. It was connected to its charger. She went over and picked it up. Anna hadn't opened any emails or texts all day. Maybe the battery had died on her and she just left it there to charge.

Cristina became a little concerned. She tried to think of when she had last seen her. The two of them had been out late the night before, partying, but they came home together and neither had been too drunk. Cristina figured Anna had gone for her usual ridiculously early morning run and then came home, showered and went to class. She checked her desk. Her backpack was sitting under it. So she must have gone to class, come back to the room and gone out from there. Maybe she was just down the hall, hanging out with some of their friends.

She checked around. No one had seen her all day. In fact, one of the girls said that Anna hadn't been at an economics class they took together.

Cristina was tempted to call Anna's mom in Washington. She'd met Anna's parents and really liked Mrs. Smithers. The senator seemed nice, but he was always so busy or preoccupied that she didn't really feel she knew him. But she did know Mrs. Smithers and knew she was a worrier. Calling her would only upset her, probably senselessly. She decided to wait.

She and some friends headed over to the SAE fraternity house for a Friday afternoon party. Some of the guys there had classes with Anna too. No one had seen her all day.

At 8 pm, Cristina decided she couldn't wait any longer. She went back to the dorm and tried to find her corridor's Resident Assistant. But it was Friday at 8 and the RA was nowhere to be found. She considered calling someone at the university or campus security, but just wasn't sure. At about nine, she was able to track down the RA and tell her that no one had seen Anna since the night before.

The RA immediately called her superior who called up the chain to the Dean of Students. Normally the calls wouldn't have gone that far after a co-ed had only been missing for about fifteen hours, but this wasn't just any co-ed. This was the senior senator from the state of Montana's daughter and she was a student at the University of Montana.

By 9:30, there were security officers in Anna and Cristina's room.

They questioned Cristina and the few other girls who were in at that early hour on a Friday night. Cristina explained that she thought she remembered her roommate getting up at about 6 that morning, or some ungodly early hour and going for a run, as she always did, but she wasn't positive. That was the last time anyone even thought they'd seen her.

At 11 pm, Cristina called Mrs. Smithers.

Within thirty minutes the University President and the head of campus security were in their room. They didn't find her body until Sunday.

Chapter 34

As soon as Agent Ready heard that a senator's daughter was missing, even before they found her body, he knew he had another victim. By that time, there was a three-day-old bureau task force looking into the previous murders. In addition to the three Chief Mason uncovered, the task force came up with a probable fourth in Georgia. The senator's daughter would be the fifth.

The decision not to warn members of Congress of threats to their families was well above Ready's pay grade, so at least he didn't have that heat to bear. Still he had plenty of his own.

Chapter 35

The media reaction to the Smithers murder and the subsequent media commentary on the likely link to the murder of Senator Thompson's mother was bound to lead some enterprising reporters to investigate that connection and discover the other related murders. The Feds and the Obama administration wouldn't want that to happen. They would want to control it.

He wanted to control it too. At first, he thought he would alert the media, so that the politicians wouldn't be able to spin the story of the killings their own way. But before he did, before he laid out his agenda, he wanted to get through the next three killings. And as he thought about it, he realized that the more they spun the news, the more he could embarrass them.

Chapter 36

They named her Jane. She quickly became the focal point of their lives. While they made the same mistakes most parents make with their first infant and spent her first three months in an exhausted fog, Greg and Sarah had never been happier.

A year after Jane's birth, Sarah developed endometrial cancer and had a radical hysterectomy. She was to be their only child. But there was never a time when they felt they shortchanged. Their daughter was everything to them.

The upholstery business was going well enough that Sarah was able to stay home to take care of Jane. With two doting grandmothers, she could have easily have gone back to work, but it wasn't what she wanted.

Their lives settled into a happy if somewhat stereotypical routine. Greg worked hard, but he enjoyed running and growing Hopper Upholstery. When he was away from the business, he was generally able to forget about it. They were a young family having fun.

Chapter 37

The South Carolina killing would be the easiest of the next three. His target was the sixty-eight year old sister of the senior senator from New York. The senator, Adam Keating, was in his third term and was well known as the least camera-shy politician on the hill. There was no tragedy too small for Adam to express his heartfelt sympathy on the evening news. His sister's name was Eleanor Morton. She was a retired university professor who had spent most of her adult life in Manhattan during the school year and in Paris during the summer. Watching her had been difficult, but killing her would be relatively easy.

Dr. Morton retired to Myrtle Beach and bought a small house on a quiet residential street. Her street dead-ended in front of the house and a small canal ended behind it. Her lot and the canal were heavily wooded on the dead end side and on the side of the canal across from Eleanor's house, so access would be easy. The hard part was watching her without being seen. The woods across the canal from her backyard were only about twenty to thirty feet deep. Those woods backed up to a commercial area, and the lot immediately across the canal from Eleanor's was a busy motorcycle shop. There was no way he could hang around in the parking lot or hide in the thin strip of woods between it and the canal without being seen, at least not during the shop's regular hours, which were from 9 to 5 Monday through Saturday. Those hours would have left him plenty of time to watch her, but the motorcycle shop's back parking lot was a popular hangout for some of the bikers. They often partied there for a few hours after closing. They used to stay even later, until all hours of the night, but ironically, Eleanor and some of her neighbors complained to the police and they pushed the bikers out.

Consequently, at night he had access to a secluded vantage point across the canal from the back of her house and, when he was ready, to the house itself.

To observe her, he parked at a busy strip mall about a half-mile away from the bike shop and simply went for a late night walk. After 9 pm, there wasn't much traffic and he could easily time his pace so that he could duck into the woods at the end of the canal when there weren't any cars approaching. From there, he would follow near the canal's bank, under the cover of the woods, to a spot behind the bike shop and across from Eleanor's house.

Her house, like many in the flood prone area, was built on stilts. It was essentially a cool-looking, one story ranch house, built fifteen feet above the ground. There were steps in front of the house, but those were well lit and in view of her neighbors. Under the house, where she parked her car, she'd installed an elevator. It was secure and waterproof and she could lock it at night. She thought she was relatively safe, but really all he had to do was climb one of the pillars in the back of her house to the porch there and then get in through one of the three sliding glass doors that provided access to the porch. Getting inside would be easy.

He planned to watch her for two nights. From his position in the woods, the sliding glass doors provided a good view of the inside of most of her house. With the protection of the woods, Eleanor must have felt she had privacy and didn't need to draw her blinds. But she didn't know he was there.

On the second night of his watch, Eleanor had a friend to dinner. She and the friend, another mature woman, were inside finishing dinner and their wine when he first arrived. After dinner, they moved out to the screened-in portion of her back porch, off of what appeared to be her study. They sat smoking and sipping more wine. He was surprised how clearly their voices carried across the water. They both seemed to be in good spirits, and Eleanor, who didn't have to drive anywhere, seemed a little tipsy.

He decided to alter his plan.

After about thirty minutes, the two women went back into the house, bringing their glasses and the wine bottle. It was a cool night, so Eleanor didn't have her air conditioner on. She closed the sliding screen door between the screened-in porch and her study, but not the glass slider.

Her friend left at 10:15 and Eleanor cleaned up and then settled into bed. She read for about an hour, smoking in bed and nursing another glass of wine, then went to sleep. At about 1:30, she got up and went into the bathroom for a few minutes, then went right back to bed.

He waited thirty more minutes. When he was sure she was asleep, he reached into his backpack and took out a black, loose fitting jump suit and black latex gloves. He put them on and made his way around the end of the canal, towards her backyard.

Chapter 38

Agent Ready sat with Senator Smithers and his wife in a conference room of the University Hotel. Ready had only been on the ground in Montana for about thirty minutes before he was summoned and sent to talk with the grieving, shocked parents. The Director himself had called and instructed Ready and the Western States Regional Director, Vern Narback, to brief the senator and his wife on what they suspected had happened. The Director said he had had discussions at the highest level, which Ready took to mean with President Obama, and they had decided that in the next twenty-four to forty-eight hours, they would likely go public with the idea that there might be a serial killer out there, targeting congressional relatives.

Ready was sure that the press would be way ahead of that, so the administration must have decided to let it come out that way. By having Ready brief the Smithers, they could at least front run the press with the powerful senator.

Narback, a horrible little worm of a man who clawed his way to the top over the backs of hard working agents, left it to Ready to explain the situation to the senator and his wife. The conversation hadn't gone well. Once the Smithers realized that the FBI knew a serial killer was targeting congressional family members and that they hadn't warned them in time to save their daughter, there was nothing the agent could say to console them. And truthfully, Ready couldn't blame them.

Chapter 39

The years after Jane's birth flew by. She grew into a cute, fun-loving little girl. Once she started school, Sarah went back to teaching and Greg continued to run the upholstery business.

The business was going well, better than it ever had under his father, but Greg was supporting his mom, one of his sisters and his own family, so he never felt truly financially secure. Still, everyone was doing well and with Sarah's income and health benefits, they were more than able to make ends meet. But they knew how expensive college would be, so they started planning and saving early, and were always careful with their money.

One afternoon when Jane was ten, Sarah was driving her from school to a dance class. Sarah saw a moving van up ahead of her, trying to make a left onto the street she was on, Ponus Ridge. She slowed and eventually came to a full stop as the truck driver tried to negotiate the turn. He inched forward and backwards several times, slowly gaining a better angle. By the time the driver was on his third attempt, there were three cars behind Sarah and several in the opposite lane, all waiting. Sarah put her car into park.

Finally the truck driver was able to execute the turn and move forward, towards and past Sarah's five year old Volkswagen Jetta. But as the cab passed, the trailer was still at too much of an angle to cleanly make the turn. The truck driver turned slowly into Sarah's lane to pull the trailer forward and ultimately into its proper lane. The drivers behind Sarah saw that the truck driver needed more room and all three backed up, so that he could finally complete the wide turn. The truck's cab was behind just Sarah's car and the back of the trailer was in front of her, so she couldn't move. She and Jane simply waited.

The truck driver continued forward, inching his cab further past Sarah's car and into her lane with the trailer following and moving into its proper lane. He increased his speed slightly and pulled the cab back into his lane. As he pulled forward the tail of the trailer followed, but was still partly in Sarah's lane. Sarah and Jane sat watching as the lower, back part of the trailer and the two back left tires moved into and then up onto the left front fender and then the hood of Sarah's car. The tires were half way up the hood, approaching the windshield and the passenger area of the car before the truck driver realized what happening. While he was moving slowly, he was still going too quickly for Sarah to be able to do anything other than honk her horn. She leaned over, trying to protect Jane, but thought that in a matter of seconds, they would both be crushed. Fortunately the truck driver slammed on his breaks and came to a complete stop.

Passengers in the lane behind the truck, including two off duty fireman, witnessed the slow accident and were out of their cars, running towards the Jetta almost immediately. They helped Jane and Sarah from the car, both through Jane's door, and tried to calm them. Neither was injured, but both were shaken up, especially Sarah.

Within a few minutes, the police were at the scene, comforting Sarah and taking statements from the relevant parties and the witnesses from the surrounding cars. By the time Greg arrived, about thirty minutes later, the police had a good idea of what had happened.

The senior officer at the scene, Sergeant James Cowan, assured Greg that his wife had done nothing wrong and that the truck driver would be charged with making an illegal turn. A flatbed came and took Sarah's crumpled Jetta. Officer Cowan told Greg to take his family home and that his report would show that Sarah was not at fault in any way. The truck driver was entirely responsible for the accident.

Confident that the truck driver's insurance company would be liable for the extensive damages to Sarah's car, Greg took his family from the scene of the accident to Sarah's mom's house, where they all had dinner.

When they got home at about 8 o'clock that night, there was a message on their landline to call Officer Cowan.

Greg called and Cowan said, "Mr. Hopper, I am calling to inform you that we found that there was no fault by either party in the accident that occurred today on Ponus Ridge Road."

Greg was flabbergasted. "No fault? What happened to the illegal turn you charged the driver with three hours ago? I saw you writing the ticket."

"Sir, there is no fault. The driver of the truck said that your wife's vehicle was moving at the time of the accident."

"Moving? She was parked there. She had been for about three minutes as he negotiated the turn."

"There is no proof of that, Mr. Hopper."

"No proof? There were witnesses. Did you talk to them? Did you talk to the two firemen?"

"What firemen? Do you have their names?"

Greg was furious and raised his voice into the phone. "Do I have their names? Why would I get their names? You pointedly told me that my wife was not at fault. Even if she was moving, which she wasn't, his truck ran over her car and almost crushed them in her lane. How could she possibly be at fault? Are you crazy?"

Cowan listened then coldly replied, "Look Mr. Hopper, I didn't have to call you. I am doing this as a courtesy."

"A courtesy? You are lying through your teeth. You know you told me that my wife did nothing wrong."

"Mr. Hopper, as I said, I didn't have to call you. I am not going to be insulted. Good night."

Before Greg could respond, he hung up. Sarah stood looking at him, having pieced together most of the conversation.

"I can't believe this. How can he simply lie like this?"

Greg went through the conversation in more detail with Sarah and the two of them were in shock. Until that moment, they had both believed in the law and felt that there was right and there was wrong.

"Let's go talk to him or his boss. Let's go right now."

They got a neighbor to watch Jane and drove to the Police Station. Greg approached the duty officer who was sitting behind a bulletproof glass window. The protection seemed way over the top in the quiet suburban town.

"I'd like to speak with the senior officer here please."

The policeman looked up, taking his time. "What is this in reference to?"

"My wife was involved in an… her car was run over by a truck earlier today."

"Did you report the accident at the time?"

"Yes. That's why I want to talk to the chief or whoever the senior person on duty is. Right now."

"That would be Sergeant Cowan, but he's busy. I'm sure I can handle it for you."

Greg didn't like the officer's tone or his attitude.

"I'd like to speak to Officer Cowan. Now."

"As I said, he is not available. What can I …"

"We'll wait. Please tell him Mr. and Mrs. Hopper are here." With that, Greg and Sarah walked away from the window and sat in the waiting area.

Twenty minutes later, Officer Cowan came out from behind the locked door. The Hoppers rose and met him before he was three steps into the room.

"Can I help you?"

Greg spoke. "Yes. We'd like an explanation."

"An explanation?"

Greg was argumentative from the start. "Yes. What happened? When we left you said it was clearly the truck driver's fault and that you were giving him a ticket. Now you tell us that there was no fault?"

"Yes, sir. In talking with the driver, it became clear that your wife's vehicle was moving at the time of the accident."

"I was not moving. My car was in park."

"That's not what the truck driver said."

Sarah looked at him in shock and disbelief. "Even if I was moving... which I was not, I was in park. But even if I was moving that truck ran over the front of my car and came within feet of crushing my daughter and me in our lane. Is it legal for a truck to drive into the opposite lane and run over a car? Whether that car is moving or not? And I wasn't moving. I was in park."

"None of that is clear, ma'am."

"Not clear? When you came to the scene that truck was parked on top of my car in my lane. How much more clear could it be?"

Greg, who let his wife finish but was ready to punch the officer, went on. "You told us you were giving him a ticket for an illegal turn. You told us it was clear that we were not at fault in any way."

Cowan let them finish. When they both paused he said, "Look, I didn't have to call you this evening. As I told you before, I did it as a courtesy."

"A courtesy? Are you kidding? What's courteous about calling us and lying? What happened? Did the driver pay you off?"

Cowan was getting angry too now. "Mr. Hopper, watch what you say."

"Watch what I say? Watch what you say. You know damn well that guy was entirely in the wrong. You said so. Now you are telling us that it's not clear who was at fault. What are we supposed to conclude other than that you were paid off after we left? Did you talk to the witnesses? To the two firemen who were there? Who witnessed the entire thing?"

"I'm not going to stand here and listen to this any more."

Greg stepped closer, not letting Cowan walk away. "Did you talk to the firemen?"

"What firemen? Do you have their names? Their numbers?" He smirked.

The door to the interior offices opened and the duty officer came out, stepping between the Hoppers and Cowan, but clearly siding with Cowan.

"Look folks, I suggest you calm down."

Greg stepped forward again, getting in the duty officer's face. "Do you know what is going on here? This 'policeman' is standing here smugly, blatantly lying to us." His tone was venomous.

The officer stepped forward as well.

Before things got any further out of hand, Sarah yelled, "Stop it. Both of you."

Both men stepped back. She was crying. She turned her attention to Cowan.

"How can you stand here and lie like this? You know perfectly well that I was in my lane and you know from talking to the other people there that we were all waiting for several minutes for the truck to make the turn. He went back and forth three or four times before he was able to turn. I was in park in my lane and the back of his truck ran over the front of my car. I thought he was going to crush my little daughter and me."

She broke into full out tears. Greg took her in his arms. Looking over her shoulder, he calmly said to Cowan, "You should be ashamed of yourself. You know you are lying right now."

The other officer looked at the Hoppers and knew they were probably telling the truth. In turn, the Hoppers could see he knew. Nonetheless the officer said, "Look sir, nothing is going to be solved like this. Why don't you folks just go on home?"

They left, shocked to know that they were entirely in the right but that it didn't matter.

Chapter 40

Once he was in her yard, he waited in the corner by the canal for a minute to be sure no one was moving on the street in front of her house. Then he hurried across her small back lawn, easily climbed up one of the pillars supporting the back porch and made his way into the screened-in porch and then into her den.

He quietly wiped the rubber soles of his black running shoes on the area rug in the den so that they wouldn't squeak on her wooden floors.

The living room and kitchen were an open area with a breakfast counter separating the kitchen. He planned to go into the kitchen area to get a knife, but just as he got to the opening by the counter she walked out from her bedroom, heading towards the bathroom. They were only five feet apart.

Eleanor was still half asleep and sensed him before she saw him, so initially she was more confused than afraid. He just reacted, running to her and spinning her so that he held her against him from behind. With his right arm across her chest and his right hand holding her left shoulder, he held her tight to him. He reached in front of her with his left arm and grabbed her head and spun it forcefully forward and to the left. He felt her neck crack. She sagged to the floor and died.

He walked back to her study, climbed down the pillar and walked in darkness to the woods. He then removed his dark coveralls and gloves, put them in his backpack and walked back to his car. Five hours later, he was at a rest stop in Georgia.

Chapter 41

Over the years, Hopper developed a few relationships with decorators who specialized in commercial projects. One, a woman named Mary Roycroft, became very successful. Like Greg and his father, she'd started small, doing mostly residential decorating. But she was savvy and cultivated commercial clients when she could. As her business developed, her clientele evolved from restaurants and small offices to small hotels. She had great taste, was smart and tough, and did what she was supposed to do; she worked hard to help her clients choose tasteful, functional, appropriate solutions. Once they decided what they wanted, she worked like a dog on her client's behalf to get their jobs done on time, to specs and on budget.

Roycroft used Hopper Upholstery many times. For some of her projects, especially as her business grew, Greg needed to bring in extra help to meet the scale of her demands. She knew she was stretching his capacity, and stayed on top of him to be sure he stayed on schedule, but she also knew he was reliable. On occasion, she even helped him secure the financing he needed to purchase the fabrics for the bigger jobs. Mary's newest project, her biggest by far, was to help the famous New York City real estate developer, Reggie Reynolds, with a new casino he was building in Ocean City, New Jersey. Reynolds' team hired Mary to decorate the public areas of the casino and she in turn gave Greg the job of upholstering the chairs and couches in the casino's lobbies, restaurants and convention rooms. The scope was more than ten times larger than anything he had done before. There were 7,400 chairs and over 1,200 couches. When Mary first approached him, while he wanted to do it, he almost said no. It was simply a bigger project than he had ever considered. But the work itself, especially the work on the chairs, wasn't technical. He would have to hire and train new employees, and lease additional work and storage space, but if he built in all of those costs, and charged accordingly, he could make more money than he ever dreamed possible. Additionally, Reynolds' project was in its early stages, so he would have at least sixteen months to get the work done.

He and his mother and their accountant, Renata Howard, went over the numbers again and again. They built a plan of all that they would need, the time it would take to do it, and then started to look for space to lease, to accurately price out the project. Greg figured that if he took half to two thirds of his existing upholsterers and put them on the Reynolds job, and had them teach and supervise new hires, he could use his remaining workers to keep his existing clients and decorators happy. That way, he wouldn't lose his current clients while he was working on the Reynolds project.

The potential profits were huge. Mary and Reynolds' people would be very price sensitive and would insist on a cost plus pricing, but they would allow him at least a 20% markup. On top of that, only he and his team would know the true costs. Conservatively, they believed they could net over $600,000 on the project and maybe as much a $1,000,000. That was three times more than they had ever made in a single year. But the risks were staggering. He would have to lease space, hire and train additional employees and, most significantly, pay for the fabric upfront. Mary said that Reynolds' people wanted to handle the purchase of the furniture and that it would be delivered to Hopper's warehouse. Without that, the scale of financing might have been beyond Greg's reach. Even with it, the numbers were difficult. Still, he could earn $600,000, at least. That would be more than enough to pay for Jane's college education.

Chapter 42

The next day, he had breakfast in a little diner near the motel where he'd spent the night. The morning news shows still had reporters in Missoula. By that evening, he hoped the anchors would be in Myrtle Beach.

Early on, the reporters were only talking about Smithers and Thompson. But by 8 am a story in a mid-sized Pennsylvania newspaper, *The Erie Star*, was being cited across all the networks and cable news stations. A reporter for that paper, Mike Williams, uncovered three additional killings of congressional family members. The murders, which started in January, occurred over a period of about six months and had taken place in Pennsylvania, Georgia, Illinois and, most recently, in Connecticut and Montana. They hadn't found Dr. Morton's body yet.

He was pleased to see that a smaller paper was the first to put it all together, publicly at least, and was finally satisfied with the extent of the media coverage. But he knew things would be more difficult from here on in – especially since he had yet to kill a congressional spouse. He wanted to act fast, before protection was put in place for close family members.

Chapter 43

Agent Ready's life became a living hell. He was spending so much time dealing with his superiors and frantic elected officials that he wasn't making much real progress.

In the woods near the University of Montana, investigators found footprints that may have belonged to the murderer, but there were so many prints and tracks from the kids in the search party who initially found the body that is was difficult to be sure. They also found the place on the running trail where Anna had been stopped, they thought with a trip wire, and then strangled. But there were no clues to go with it. It was the first time the killer apparently used his own murder weapon, but in this case he didn't leave it behind with the body.

One thing that had changed was that there were no false leads being left behind. Ready speculated that this meant the killer no longer had the time to find materials to plant and implicate or at least embarrass local politicians. Ready hoped that also meant he was more rushed and, hopefully, more likely to make mistakes. So far, he hadn't made any.

The agent didn't really know much more than what Matt Mason, the police chief from Harrison, Pennsylvania, had told him two weeks earlier. Some lunatic was out there killing the relatives of long-serving congressmen and senators.

In Missoula and its surrounding area and in the other cities and towns where murders occurred, agents and police officers collected information about guests who checked out of local hotels and motels on the day of or within a day or two of the murders, looking for common names or anomalies. While they had yet to find any consistent names, in Missoula at a Motel 6, a man checked in using the name Joe Helms. Helms paid in cash, used a prepaid Visa card for the security deposit and used a fictitious Idaho Springs address. Ready was sure that the name was a fake as well. He was trying to track down the Visa card but doubted it would lead anywhere.

The one possible lead they had came from the surveillance camera covering the front desk of the hotel. The tapes corresponding to Helms' check-in time showed an over-weight Caucasian male with long dark hair and a beard, wearing a baseball cap and dark glasses. The man appeared to be hunched over so even determining his height was difficult. Ready suspected this might be the man he was looking for, but doubted anything about the image was accurate. They questioned the staff about him, but no one remembered seeing him except at the time of his check-in. His room was clean.

Chapter 44

The Florida murder was by far his riskiest. His target was the former wife of Representative David Sanford, a relatively long-serving congressman from the 2nd District on the western panhandle in Panama City. Congressman Sanford left his wife Joan and their two children for a young staffer. He considered targeting the representative's new wife, but she lived in Miami Beach and logistically that posed travel problems that Panama City did not. He liked the idea that Sanford had "only" been in the House for thirteen years. His message would soon be out and he wanted to make it clear that any time over six years was too long. He felt sure that the press would be sympathetic to the ex-wife and might even blame the congressman for not protecting her while he protected his new, younger trophy wife.

Mrs. Sanford the former, who now went by her maiden name, Sinclair, lived on the fourteenth floor of an eighteen-story beachfront high rise. The building faced the street on one side and the Gulf of Mexico on the other. Each floor had five apartments. The three center ones opened on the street side and the two end apartments opened on the building's sides. The street side had open-air hallways that lead from one end of the building to the other. Every floor looked the same. There were floor to chest high, ivory-colored stucco walls, three apartment doors and big sheet glass windows in the middle, and elevators at one end of the hallways and utility rooms and a stairwell at the other. The outer hallway walls, which acted as railings, were about four feet high and were meant to protect both people and objects from falling from the higher floors to the ground below. The two apartments that opened on either side of the building were accessed by the same hallway, which ran around the ends of the building and halfway back to the Gulf side. At the corners, the hallways ran inside large structural supports that housed elevator banks on one side and utility closets and the stairway on the other. Mrs. Sinclair's apartment was on the side past the utility closet and stairwell.

To get to her apartment, she had to walk from the far corner with the elevators, past the three front-side opening apartments and then around the corner to her own apartment. He felt that if he waited either in the utility closet or on the side of the building beside it, he could simply surprise her and throw her over the side. The tricky part would be getting in and not being seen as he waited or when he tossed her.

Chapter 45

Mrs. Sinclair spent most of the year living alone. Her two kids were both in college and, since the divorce when she moved from their house into the condo, her life had lapsed into a dull routine. She still had privileges at the local country club and on Tuesday afternoons she typically played golf with three other women, then ate dinner in the club's taproom. That night she and her friends discussed the murders of congressional relatives and, in light of the murder of the senator's daughter out in Montana, what precautions were being taken for her own kids at school. She thought, but didn't verbalize, that it would be nice if the killer took out her ex's new bimbo wife.

Chapter 46

His target, Mrs. Sinclair, left her apartment at 1:20 dressed in golf clothes. He watched from his car in a shopping center parking lot, across the street from her building. She walked along the open hallway from her end of the fourteenth floor to the elevator bank at the other end.

Like many Florida high-rises, Mrs. Sinclair's building was built on pillars. The pillars provided protection from tidal flooding and easy parking for the building's tenants. A few minutes after he saw her step into the elevator, he watched a gray Chevy Tahoe pull out from the parking lot. Mrs. Sinclair was driving. He pulled out of the shopping center and followed her along Front Beach Road. There was a fair amount of traffic, but he had no problem trailing her. After about ten minutes and a few turns, she pulled into the Panama City Country Club. He kept going.

If she was playing golf, he figured he had at least a few hours. He drove back toward her apartment building. The gulf side of her road, Front Beach, was built up with luxury high-rises and the inland side was a combination of strip malls and one to two story, low-end motels. He pulled into a strip mall several buildings west of Mrs. Sinclair's building and parked.

After a while he left his car and walked further west on Front Beach along the sidewalk. He was wearing long black board shorts, a faded navy blue tee shirt, a baseball cap, dark glasses and a fake beard, and carried a backpack. About a half mile from her building, he crossed the street and cut between two buildings along a public access way to the beach. Then he made his way back east, to a spot behind her building. It was about 3:40 and the crowds had thinned out, but not so much so he would be particularly noticeable. The tide was in and the beach behind her apartment was relatively narrow, about three hundred feet from the water to the low outer perimeter wall of her building. He positioned himself on the soft sand just past the beach access door from her building. He took a towel from his backpack and spread it facing away from the wind, and towards the southwest. From there he could watch the door as he pretended to read.

After about forty minutes two pale kids came out of the building, bounding towards the water. Seconds later a well-tanned elderly woman, who must have been their grandmother, followed them. She watched the kids, two boys who looked to be about fifteen and thirteen, for a few minutes. She gave them some instructions and went back inside.

An hour later, the boys started to gather their towels. He picked up his towel and walked back to the access door of the building. He walked slowly with his back to the boys, pretending to be distracted and searching for something in his pockets and backpack. He stopped right by the door, by the security keypad, and started searching in earnest. The boys came up to the door and looked up to him.

The older boy asked, "Did you lose something, mister?"

He kept his face turned down, his features largely hidden by his baseball cap's visor, and looked up through dark sunglasses. In as non-threatening a voice as possible he responded, "I can't find my reading glasses. They're only $15 drugstore glasses, but I just had them."

He watched through the dark lenses as the boy punched in the security code. 2547.

"I must have left them on the beach. Have a good one, guys."

The younger boy said, "You, too. Hope you find your glasses."

He walked back to the beach to the spot where he had been sitting and pretended to search for his glasses. A few minutes later, he walked back to the building. He put one finger of a skin tone latex glove over his index finger and punched the code: 2547. The lock disengaged and he opened the door, gaining access to the open parking area. Across the parking area, he saw two entry points to the building above, the elevator bank and the stairwell, which was on Mrs. Sinclair's side of the building. He opted for the stairwell. As he walked through the parking garage, he figured there might be security cameras so he kept his head down and walked a little hunched over, as if he had bad posture. At the fire door of the stairwell, he again punched in the security code and then made his way up to the fourteenth floor. By the fifth floor, he figured he would be unlikely to bump into anyone in the stairwell and relaxed.

By the time he got to the fourteenth floor, he was a little winded, but really pleased with the configuration of the building. The stairs opened into a utility room on the right front corner of the building, about twelve feet from Mrs. Sinclair's apartment. Inside the utility room was a garbage shoot, some recycling bins and locked electrical boxes. There was also a small window in the door between the utility room and the exterior hallway that provided a good view of the hallway. He could wait for the congressman's ex-wife there. If someone else came down the hall, he could go into the stairwell and slowly walk down. If they followed, he would simply walk all the way down and Mrs. Sinclair would live. If they just dropped off their garbage, he would wait a minute or two, then go back into the utility room.

Two people dumped their garbage over the next few hours, both uneventfully. As he waited, it occurred to him that she might have returned while he was on the beach. If she did, she saved her own life.

At 9:30, he heard the ding of the elevator door opening at the other end of the open hallway. As he watched through the window, from the back of utility room, Mrs. Sinclair walked out of the elevator. She was alone. He waited until she walked by and then just as she passed the door and turned down the hallway on her side of the building, he opened the door and went right to her. Without hesitating, he simply picked her up and threw her over the balcony. She screamed, but just like that, she was gone.

He didn't even look over the balcony to see her fall. He went back into the utility room, picked up his backpack and hurried down the steps. Then he went through the parking lot, out the back door to the beach, down the beach and back to his car.

Chapter 47

By noon the next morning, Ready was in Panama City. This time, for the first time, he had some real evidence.

Mrs. Sinclair's body was found at 5:40 that morning. A third floor resident of her building saw her body from his hallway as he was leaving for work. She had jumped, fallen or, everyone suspected, been pushed, most likely from the hallway outside of her apartment.

Local agents and the Panama City police canvassed the building and neighboring buildings and reviewed recordings from the security cameras in Mrs. Sinclair's building. It was from those tapes that Ready got his first real break. A man in long swim trunks and a tee shirt entered the parking garage from the beach entrance at 5:02. Through their canvassing, agents discovered that two Canadian boys, Alan and Andrew Eaton, who were visiting their grandmother, had spoken with a man at the beach access door. The man told the boys that he had left his glasses on the beach, but Ready suspected he had somehow gotten the access code from them. The tapes showed that a few minutes after the boys came in, the man in the long trunks entered from the same beach access door and walked through the parking garage to the stairwell. He entered the security code there and went inside.

Ready, his crew and the forensic team went over the stairwell, the utility room and the hallway on Mrs. Sinclair's floor with expected scrutiny. They were running the multitude of prints they found, but Ready doubted it would lead to anything. The killer was too careful. Ready surmised that he'd waited in the utility room, watching the hallway for Mrs. Sinclair. When she came home – the security camera had her entering the elevator at 9:28 – he'd probably watched her come down the hallway towards him and her apartment. Ready suspected that after she passed, he simply opened the door, grabbed her and threw her over.

The garage tapes showed the same man who entered from the beach that afternoon exiting from the stairwell back into the garage at 9:38. He made his way from the stairwell back to the beach door and out into the night. Coming in and going out of the garage, he walked hunched over, trying to hide his true height in an area in which he probably knew he was being filmed. But the Eaton boys thought he was about 6 feet tall. The older of the two, Alan, was 5′10″ and he said the man at the door was two or three inches taller than he was.

The tapes didn't show much of his face, he wore a hat and dark glasses, but at least they had an image. They compared the images they found on the Panama City tapes with the Missoula tape and using facial recognition technology, confirmed that both images were probably of the same man, in spite of apparent differences in weight, hair color and even gait. With the data they had, they could at least try to pick him out of crowds all over the country.

Chapter 48

Jane was a senior in high school and was accepted at Middlebury College in rural Vermont. Greg and Sarah both were so proud of her. She had Sarah's intellect and joy for life and Greg's dogged determination.

Paying for Middlebury was going to be a stretch. While Greg and Sarah lived modestly, life in the shadow of New York City was expensive. On top of that, Sarah's mom had a very rare strain of ovarian cancer and while she did have insurance, it was a pretty basic plan. Because her cancer was so unusual, her doctors tried a variety of different treatments. Individual shots of one particular medication that her doctors recommended cost over $1,500 per shot. The insurance company would not approve it, calling it experimental and untested, but Sarah's mother's doctors were confident it would be helpful, so Sarah and Greg authorized its use. They gave her eight of those shots.

She also had thirty-five days of radiation. It had been a brutal regimen and she was hospitalized for the last seven days of her treatment. The insurance company recommended that she postpone the treatment to regain her strength, but she wanted to bear down and get it over with. As a result, the costs incurred during the hospitalization were only partially covered. And finally, the combination of the radiation treatments and hospitalization had been so draining that she had to spend six weeks in a live-in care center, to regain her strength.

The treatments did work. She was cancer free and pretty much her old self, but all in, it cost Greg and Sarah about $68,000. They took most of the money, a large chunk of their savings, from Jane's college fund. As a result, the fund was well short of where they intended it to be. And they underestimated the cost of tuition. When they started planning years earlier, they thought she would go to a state school for $20,000 to $25,000 per year. Their financial advisors had made it clear that the costs would continue to go up over the years, so they tried to set aside enough for up to $30,000 per year. Middlebury's cost was a staggering $62,350 per year. Even without the unexpected medical costs, it would have been a stretch. With those costs, it seemed impossible.

So while the Reynolds casino project involved a great deal of financial risk, it seemed like the easiest and maybe only way out of their troubles. They took out a second mortgage and signed the lease for the larger facility required for the project. The fabric companies also provided financing. Hopper Upholstery took on more debt than Greg had ever imagined possible. But all he had to do was to make delivery on time and the revenues would more than cover the expenses and Jane's tuition.

Chapter 49

The next two murders would be quick. In Arizona, he made another statement.

After the horrific school shooting at the Sandy Hook Elementary School in Connecticut, Congress failed to pass even the most watered-down gun control legislation. Parents of the victims of the school shooting had pressed Congress and Connecticut law makers for three things: a ban on assault rifles, a ban on the sale of ammunition clips or magazines holding more than a still staggeringly high twenty rounds and a mandatory waiting period for a gun license – which many states issued at the time of purchase – so that background checks could be performed. Polls showed that an incredible 90% of voters favored the legislation. Connecticut passed a softened version of the legislation that the victims' parents found acceptable. But, in spite of an overwhelming national mandate for gun control, the United States Congress did nothing more than talk. They couldn't even pass a mandatory waiting period for background checks. Such was the power of the NRA.

In Arizona, three hours before he shot and killed a US senator's brother, he walked into a gun shop and purchased an assault rifle. He filled out the license application form using his wrong hand and a false identity. After he completed the form he asked the sales clerk to get him two thirty round ammo clips. While the clerk fetched the clips, he wiped his prints from the application form.

He taped his copy of the form to the butt of the rifle, which he left beside the body at the victim's ranch.

Chapter 50

Mike Williams was *The Erie Star* reporter who first broke the story of the Congressional Killer. He had received a great deal of attention since his story was released. But neither he nor anyone else really knew why the murderer was doing what he was doing.

When his mail was delivered on Friday afternoon, Mike got the answer. After the story was published, he received dozens of letters and emails every day and this Friday was no different. Many of the letters were related to the murders and many of the writers claimed to be the killer. On that Friday, one envelope caught his attention. It was postmarked from Panama City, Florida, and the date on the postmark was August 5th, the day Mrs. Sinclair was killed. She was killed that night, so this letter must have been mailed before she had been murdered.

He carefully opened it, using a letter opener and touching only the corners of the letter.

Dear Mr. Williams,

For decades now, elected officials in this country have put their own interest in being re-elected and obtaining personal power and wealth above the interests of the citizens they are elected to represent and serve.

Since the time of the Romans, politicians have been corrupt and inwardly focused. And yet in election after election, year after year, incumbents are re-elected. Disenfranchised voters have seen that term limits would go a long way towards solving the problems created by these self-interested politicians. Many who are elected go in hoping to bring about change, but once in, they are overwhelmed by the system. Re-elected incumbents run committees and control what gets voted on and what does not. Even during years of congressional upheaval like 1994 and 2010, the newly elected find that they are forced to either go along with the status quo or become isolated and totally ineffective.

Some cities and states have been able to overcome this by setting term limits, but at a national level the process required to mandate term limits is so complex and so dependent on sitting politicians at state and federal levels, that term limits will never be enacted. The only way they could be is if sitting politicians are willing to limit their own power, to consider the greater good.

It is clear that in the long run, most politicians are not able to work for the greater good. The state by state referendums required to force term limits at a national level will never happen because national and local power brokers, elected and unelected, have no interest in bringing about that change because that change will reduce their power, corrupt or not.

So something has to be done. And it is being done. For the past seven months, I have been murdering close and distant relatives of long-serving politicians. These people are totally innocent and I am a murderer. I have no right to kill them and I will eventually be caught and brought to justice, as I should be. But until I am, I will continue to kill the relatives of any sitting congressman or congresswoman who has served more than two terms and who has not formally declared that he will not seek re-election or any sitting senator who has not formally declared he will not seek re-election. They must all remove their names from the ballots. Six years is long enough.

Almost 90% of us think they are doing a terrible job. They have gotten us into wars we don't want to be in and into debt that our great-grandchildren will be paying off for decades. They can't even pass simple gun control legislation. Six years is enough.

Sitting politicians have a choice. They can step aside or they can be a party to the murder of their own relatives. I want to show these men and women for the self-serving, self-interested, selfish people they are. I think that many of them will be willing to risk their family members' lives to hold on to their power. Some will claim, perhaps correctly, that they cannot bend to the demands of a terrorist. But 90% of us think they are doing a bad job. 90%. All they have to do is let someone else try. They can save their families and help change a system that is clearly broken by simply stepping aside.

To sitting politicians, I say the following: If you care about your families, do not seek re-election. Take your name off the ballot list and I will take the names of your relatives off my list. If you think that you being in office for another term is more important than the life of your son or daughter or mother or uncle or second cousin or spouse, then run for office again. Explain to your family and to voters that you being in office is more important than them being alive.

To the people, I say the following: I know that murder is wrong and that I deserve to be punished, and I will be. But you the voter can support change without breaking the law. VOTE FOR ANYONE ELSE. THROW THE INCUMBENTS OUT. DEMAND TERM LIMITS. The incumbents have had their chance and they have failed miserably. Most ballots have the word incumbent next to currently serving elected officials. If the ballots in your city or state don't, demand that they do. Don't vote for any incumbent. We can do better than this. THROW THEM OUT. VOTE FOR ANYONE ELSE.

All that you politicians have to do is not run again and the killing stops. We can live without you. Your relatives can too.

Finally, to prove that I am who I say I am, tonight after I mail this letter, I will murder the former wife of Congressman David Sanford. She seems to be a very nice woman. She is the mother of two college-age children. Sanford, who is 57, left her to marry a 24 year old woman from his staff.

THROW THE INCUMBENTS OUT. VOTE FOR ANYONE ELSE.

Williams rechecked the postmark on the envelope. It was dated August 5th. Mrs. Sinclair's body was discovered on the morning of the 6th. Today was August 8th.

He read the letter again and then walked to his editor's office.

The editor, Michael Carver, had never been busier than he was since they published Williams' article. He and his paper were suddenly thrust into the national spotlight and were being depicted as the perfect local newspaper. He and Williams worked hard on the original story and it was good, well-researched work. He felt like Ben Bradlee of *The Washington Post* in the Watergate-era and he knew he owed it to the young reporter.

"Hey, Mike. What's up?"

"I think I just got a letter from the Congressional Killer."

Carver looked at him in shock. "You're kidding me? Really? Where is it?"

"On my desk. I don't think we should touch it any more than I already have." As he was finishing his sentence, Carver was up and leading him from his office back to his desk. *The Star*'s editorial offices were in an open layout, and Williams' desk was in the middle of the open bullpen, so when the other reporters and workers saw Carver and Williams walking so purposefully, they knew something was up.

Once they reached his desk, Carver took the seat and Williams stood behind him, looking over his shoulder. The two pages of the letter were set side by side, with the envelope placed above them. They each read. For Williams, it was his third time through.

When he got to the part where the killer mentioned planning to kill Mrs. Sinclair, Carver pointed to the passage without touching it and said, "Holy shit."

Williams responded, "I know." Then he pointed at the postmark on the envelope. "August 5th, from Panama City. That is the day she was killed. She was thrown from her balcony some time after nine on the night of the fifth. He must have mailed this that day, before the post office closed. This has to be from the killer. Don't you think?"

Carver just kept reading. Then he read it again.

When he finished he took his phone and took several pictures of each page and of the envelope.

"I think we should move this into my office."

"Yeah, I agree."

A group started to gather around Mike's desk. Carver shooed them away and he and Williams each took an empty manila folder from a stack on the desk and slid one under each page of the letter and carefully took them into Carver's office, placing them on a small conference table. Williams brought the envelope in the same way.

Carver had a staff photographer take better pictures of the document then called one of the FBI agents who'd questioned them after they published the first story.

Chapter 51

The furniture, fabric and materials were delivered to the facility Hopper had leased for the Reynolds Casino project. It took up about eighty percent of the allotted storage space.

Greg's next step was to do some tests to figure out the most efficient way to cut the fabric for each type of chair or couch that was being used. They had to be sure to use enough fabric to make the furniture's seams strong enough for commercial use without wasting material. They would fully upholster several units of each furniture item until they were confident that they were using the most cost and technically effective cutting patterns and that they were upholstering each piece to appropriate aesthetic and commercial durability standards. That process, especially developing the best cutting patterns, was an art, not a science.

After countless trials and days of discussions, they had what they thought was the best strategy. Greg's plan was to get the most cumbersome and biggest part of the job, the 7,400 chairs, done first. If an upholsterer believed he had the best cutting pattern, the most efficient way to produce a very large number of the same product was to cut the material first, then upholster the units afterwards. That was what Greg decided to do.

Chapter 52

Ready saw a copy of the letter about three hours after Williams opened it. So did President Obama. Within the administration, there had been some discussion of trying to suppress the letter, but that was the normal course of things. It was quickly agreed that even if they could get the paper to sit on it for a few days, there was no way to control the actual killer.

The next morning, *The Erie Star*, circulation 46,235, scooped every newspaper in the country for the second time in two weeks.

The reaction on the Hill was predictable. Congressmen and congresswomen and senators took their often-claimed high ground and rightly denounced the letter writer as a domestic terrorist. The network and cable news talking heads also denounced the killer, but a few discussed the issues he raised.

The pressure on the Feds to find the killer, now nationally known as the Congressional Killer, became even more intense. The two known, useable videos of the suspect, from the parking area of Mrs. Sinclair's building and from the hotel lobby in Missoula, were played on a nearly constant loop on news channels and online. With the success of the broadcasts used to identify the Tsarnaev brothers in the wake of the Boston Marathon bombings in 2013, expectations were that the release of the Congressional Killer videos would yield equally quick and favorable results. The problem was that the current videos showed two very different looking men. The man in the Missoula photo was fat and looked short. He had long dark hair, a beard and a mustache. The man in the Florida pictures looked taller and much leaner. "Expert" commentators on the news programs explained that it was harder to fake thin than fat, so they confidently proclaimed that the Florida images gave a more accurate picture of the suspect. But really all those images showed were clips of a tallish white male with long hair. To the naked eye, his facial features were nondescript.

Predictably, the letter itself gave away nothing. There were no prints other than those of Mike Williams, *The Erie Star*'s reporter. The paper the letter was printed on was cheap, printer-quality Hammermill, which is available at almost every office supply store in the country, as was the envelope, and it was closed with an adhesive strip, so there was no DNA. Even the font, Times New Roman, was among the most commonly used.

Analysts tried to break down the letter itself, to see if any of the wording or inferences provided some hint about who the killer was. It was clear from his actions that the killer felt he had been horribly wronged by the federal government and it was likely that his representative or senator was one who had been serving for a long time. Agents worked with congressional staffers and with the Secret Service to gather lists of especially unsatisfied constituents. However, with congressional approval ratings as low as they were, those lists were extremely long. The analysts also felt that if they could detect any regional influence or dialect from the letter, they could narrow their search. Because many of the murders had occurred in the eastern half of the country, they thought that the killer was probably also from the east. But nothing they read helped them narrow it down any further.

Chapter 53

It took over two weeks, but Greg and his staff finished cutting the fabric for the 7,400 chairs. Over 500 chairs were already upholstered. He and Reynolds' decorator, Mary Roycroft, were pleased with the results.

The leased space was divided into three areas. One now contained the cut fabric for the chairs and the still largely uncut fabric rolls for the 1,200 couches and love seats, and stuffing and padding materials. The second area, the biggest, contained the un-upholstered furniture and the 500 finished chairs. The third area was the work area.

Things were going perfectly. The work on the chairs was much easier than the couch work, so Greg and his regulars were training and supervising the new hires with the chairs. The couches would be more difficult, but Greg was well ahead of schedule and confident that he would have no problem making delivery.

Chapter 54

He drove from Arizona to Missouri in four days, intentionally taking a roundabout route. He spent the first night after the Arizona murder in Provo, Utah and the second and third in Sioux Falls, South Dakota.

His next target was John Gallagher, the eldest son of Missouri's senior senator. An ultra conservative, Senator Frances Gallagher was the longest-serving woman in Congress. She had four children. Her oldest son, John, lived in Kirkwood, a suburb of St. Louis, with his wife and three children. He was rumored to be considering a run for Congress himself.

On paper, Gallagher's address looked perfect. He lived in a heavily wooded area off Sugar Creek Ridge Drive in Kirkwood. He thought he could probably access the woods as a runner or on a mountain bike and observe Gallagher and his family from a well-protected spot.

He got a room at a Holiday Inn north of the city, about forty-five minutes from Kirkwood. On the day of his first visit, he intended to drive through the target's neighborhood and then park in a nearby shopping center. He purchased a cheap, used mountain bike in Sioux Falls and planned to use it to ride through the woods to observe the Gallaghers.

Their house was on a very small dead end street. He intended to drive slowly by the end of the street to get a sense of what, if any, security was apparently present. His letter to *The Erie Star* and the quick succession of killings in the past few weeks had resulted in near round the clock media coverage of the murders and consequently he felt sure that congressional relatives would be getting more and more protection.

In Arizona when he purchased the gun license and the assault rifle, he used the name Kenneth Bradley Anneywon. When he signed the application, which he subsequently taped to the rifle's stock, he signed "Ken B. Anneywon".

"Can Be Anyone" was the headline on dozens of newspapers across the country the next day. *The New York Post*'s headline read: "ANNEYONE CAN GET A GUN."

The articles and editorials in papers and blogs and the discussions among the talking heads on television took on added dimensions. It was clear that the murderer, whoever he was, purchased a semi-automatic assault weapon and several thirty round clips using a fake Oregon driver's license just hours before the murder. The national debate on gun control that emerged after the Connecticut school shooting was back in full bloom and Congress' failure to enact any legislation whatsoever after that shooting was casting new doubt about the already unpopular institution. President Obama's reluctance to push the legislation through and his silence on the issue in the months after the legislation's failure was also putting considerable pressure on the administration. The public debate went a step farther, moving to what citizens could do in the absence of congressional action. Term limits became part of that debate. Anchor after anchor explained the state-by-state referendum process that such a change would require. Everyone in the public eye was quick to repudiate the killer, but the point he was trying to make was slowly being acknowledged.

The national conversation he hoped to create was starting. But, because he was putting pressure on the established powers in a way that no one ever had before, the pressure and resources to catch him were greater than they had ever been before. Future killings would be much more difficult.

Chapter 55

Greg's mother called him on his cell phone. He was on the floor at the time, upholstering a chair.

She didn't even say hello. She simply said, "Greg, have you seen the news?"

"What news, Mom?"

"About Reynolds?"

"No, what?"

"There are rumors that he is going to declare bankruptcy on the Ocean City Casino project. They say he missed a bond payment and that bondholders are going to seize the assets."

Greg's heart sank. He was at the most vulnerable point in his project. He had already cut about 80% of the fabric he purchased, fabric that had cost over a million dollars. The 20% that was uncut still retained most of its initial value, but if Reynolds didn't take and pay for the finished chairs, the cut fabric would be worthless. Greg would be ruined. Hopper Upholstery was an LLC, so Greg and Sarah's personal assets wouldn't be touched, but those assets didn't amount to much. He invested a portion of Jane's college fund and the money from the second mortgage on their house in the Reynolds Casino project. His creditors insisted that he have considerable skin in the game.

"That can't be right. The guy's a billionaire. They talk about him on TV everyday. He has more companies and money than almost anyone in the country."

His mom's voice gave away how hurt she felt. She knew her son was ruined. "I don't understand the details. I'm just telling you what I heard on CNBC."

"Since when do you watch CNBC?" He was reaching for anything.

"Arlene told me to turn it on." Arlene was one of Greg's mom's closest friends and apparently a pretty good day trader. Greg knew she watched the markets all day long.

He could hear the devastation in his mother's voice. "Don't worry, Mom. It can't be that bad. Let me check it out. I'll call you back when I find out what's going on."

His next call was to Mary Roycroft, Reynolds' decorator for the project. The call went straight to voice mail. "Mary, it's Greg. Give me a call right away. My mother said she heard that there is some issue with Reynolds and the Ocean City Casino. She said she heard it on CNBC. Do you know anything about it? Call me. Let me know."

He hung up. He hadn't been able to repeat the words his mother used, that Reynolds might declare bankruptcy on the project. It couldn't be that bad.

Chapter 56

Ready had more information to work with. There was another video, this time of the killer in the ridiculous gun shop that sold him the license, the assault rifle and the ammunition clips. The video, which showed the shop owner and killer, was causing almost as much disdain for the idiot shop owner as it was for the killer.

The images of the killer were typically ineffective. This time he was very fat with long brown scraggily hair and a beard and mustache. He was wearing a cap and tinted glasses. It was clear that he knew where the camera was and never turned to face it directly.

The video showed him wiping the license application while the idiot was getting the ammunition clips. When he paid, he pulled a wad of cash from his wallet. He held the bills, which were all hundreds, between the thumb and index finger of his right hand. He placed the bills on the counter and spread them out with his index finger, which had a Band Aid on its tip. There were eight bills, $800. The gun, license and ammo came to $687.17. He recounted the bills, then acting as if he had miscounted, retrieved the top one that he had touched with his bare thumb, and put it back in his wallet. He left the seven untouched bills on the counter. The shop owner quickly snapped them up.

He never touched the counter and he used his own pen, a nondescript Bic. There would be no prints. He made it all look so easy. The gun shop did have a camera covering part of the parking lot, and the killer could be seen leaving the store, but he walked out of the limited range of the camera before getting into any car. The store and its parking lot were on a corner and the lot had exits to a busy street and to a quiet side street. There were other cameras on the busier street and some of those caught passing traffic. The killer took the side street.

Chapter 57

Greg dreaded the thought of calling Sarah. She called him. "Is it true?"

"Apparently some of it is. I don't know what it means for us yet."

She could tell by his voice what it meant. Before taking on the project and the second mortgage, they discussed the risk they were taking. She had been reluctant. She was always more risk averse financially than he was. But since he took over his father's business twenty-three years earlier, he had been taking risks and, until this time, things had always worked out well.

"What might it mean?"

"I'm not sure, Sarah."

"Worse case. If Reynolds declares bankruptcy?"

Greg paused. He still didn't understand much. He eventually talked to Mary and to his accountant, Renata Howard. He asked Renata how someone as rich as Reynolds could possibly be bankrupt. She explained that he wasn't personally bankrupt. It was just one of his many corporations, the Reynolds Ocean City Casino, Resort and Convention Center, that was declaring bankruptcy.

Reynolds, who had his name plastered all over everything that had anything to do with the project, including little embroidered "RR" crests in the top center of the 7,400 pieces of material Hopper and his crew had cut for the chair backs, now claimed that he had little to do with the day-to-day operations of the project. In a CNBC interview, he implied that had he not been so busy with his far flung, multi-billion dollar real estate empire, he would have been able to give the Ocean City project his full attention and things would have worked out well. As it was, while it was unfortunate, it was just a small blip and one that he would hardly feel.

Hopper couldn't believe his ears.

He responded to his wife's question. "If it is true and the Reynolds holding company building the casino does declare bankruptcy, then any of a number of things could happen. The best case, as I understand it Sarah, and I'm not sure I do, but the best case is that the bondholders in this project do something called restructuring the loans. That means that they reduce the interest rate that is paid on their bonds. I think to do that Reynolds would have to give up some or maybe all of his ownership in the project. If he just gave up part of it, I don't think it would have that big of an impact on us."

"What if he gives up all of his interest or the bond people don't want him?"

Greg thought about the "RR" crests on the backs of the chairs. He knew that if Reynolds wasn't in, the new owners wouldn't use his name and at the very least the material cut for the backs of the chairs would be useless. The loss on that material alone would totally wipe out his profits.

"I just don't know Sarah."

"What is the worst case?"

He paused. "I think the worst case would be that he and the bondholders fail to agree on a restructuring. Then the entire project goes into receivership. I think everything gets sold to pay off the creditors, the lenders, which I guess are the bondholders and the banks."

"How about us? Do we have any claim? Can we get back the money we used to buy all of that fabric? What about the money we borrowed to buy it on top of our own investment?"

He didn't want to have this conversation. It was too early. Everything was still up in the air. He decided to just try to explain everything as honestly as he could, to the best of his understanding. "With the fabric we have already cut, its value is way down. If the casino is built and it is still called Reynolds Casino, then I am sure the chairs will be used and I think we might be okay." He paused again, letting the little ray of hope sink in. "If the project closes or the creditors take over without Reynolds and change the name, then, at the very least, all of the seatbacks that we have made lose a lot, most of their value. They have the "RR" crest on the back. If it's not called the Reynolds Casino, I can't imagine the new owners will want that crest."

"Won't they have to pay us for them? For the seatback cuttings?"

"I'm just not sure. If the deal goes away, they sell assets to pay the bondholders: the land, the buildings and all of the property. From what I understand, and this could all be wrong, but from what I understand, if they start selling assets they pay off everyone Reynolds owes in a certain order. The bondholders first, then the banks and then eventually, if there is any money left, people like us."

"Will there be any money left?"

"I don't know, Sarah."

She didn't say anything. She didn't have to. They both knew that she had been quietly opposed to the whole thing.

"Can we sell the material?"

"We can sell the uncut fabric. I think we should be able to get close to what we paid for it from the manufacturers. At least, I hope so."

"How much is still uncut? I thought you had most of it done."

"We've cut about 80% of it."

"What is that worth?"

"I don't know. Not much."

"And the seat bottoms?"

"They're all cut. If Reynolds is out, then whoever owns things might finish the project. And I can imagine they would want to use the chairs and couches Reynolds already purchased and they might use the seat bottoms, unless the furniture manufacturer hasn't been paid yet. If not, then maybe the furniture company would take back the chairs. If they do, then the seat bottoms will lose most of their value too."

"So what will happen to us?"

Chapter 58

As he approached Gallagher's short street, Dunvegan Lane, he slowed to take a look. Gallagher's house, a white, center hall colonial with black shutters, was the second on the left. There was a navy sedan parked in front with two men in dark suits sitting inside. He kept driving and reassessed his plan. If there was a security presence in front of the house, he felt sure there would also be men out back and maybe even in the woods. He would have to be very careful. The authorities were smart. They would have people taking pictures of runners, bikers and maybe even cars that might be staking out congressional relatives. License plates would be checked and crosschecked. Any plate that popped up on multiple occasions would be suspect. The killings were going to be much more difficult from here on.

He decided to stay in public areas, where it would be more difficult for the authorities to single him out. Gallagher worked for a law firm in St. Louis. He decided to watch the senator's son from outside of his law office, which was in a high rise in the heart of the downtown area. The office building didn't have underground parking so Gallagher would either have to walk to his car or be picked up.

That afternoon, after bypassing Gallagher's house, he drove for about thirty minutes to a large shopping center in the northwest suburbs, near his hotel. He parked his car in the lot of the shopping center and took a bus into downtown St. Louis. At about 4:30, he found a Starbucks across the street from Gallagher's office building, bought a coffee and sat in a window seat. He was wearing khakis, a white, short-sleeved dress shirt, a gray wig and a tightly trimmed graying beard and mustache. He looked like an average, overweight, well-groomed man in his late fifties. He read *The Post Dispatch* and watched out the window.

At about 5:20, he saw two well-built men in dark suits come out of one of the three revolving doors in front of Gallagher's office building. The men scanned the plaza around the entrance and then, apparently thinking everything was clear, turned and nodded back towards the building. A moment later, Gallagher and another beefy looking guy, probably another bodyguard, came out of the building. The men surrounded Gallagher and walked him to his car. He doubted that the guards were agents. They looked a little too rough. He suspected that the senator had hired a private security firm to watch her son, who was probably and rightly viewed as a high profile target. He also suspected that the Feds had at least an agent or two watching potential targets. He consciously stopped watching Gallagher and his entourage, pointedly turning his head in the opposite direction and watching an attractive young woman walk the other way. Then he went back to reading and did not look out the window again for another ten minutes. He read for another thirty, milking his coffee and deciding on his next move. The senator's son was safe.

Chapter 59

Most of the 435 congressmen and congresswomen and 100 senators had dozens of relatives. If relatives as distant as second cousins were targets, as had been the case in Illinois, some incumbents might have as many as 50 or even 100 relatives who could be on the killer's list. The only thing that the FBI and the Secret Service really had going for them was that the incumbents held the purse strings for the protection budget. Predictably, money was flowing in the direction of the agencies. Deficits be damned, again.

There were 75 freshman and 64 sophomore congressmen and 14 freshman senators in the 113th Congress. Much to their dismay, freshman and sophomore representatives were viewed as unlikely targets and accordingly, their families were given very little protection. In light of the Congressional Killer's position that senators shouldn't serve more than one term, the 12 freshman senators were given approximately the same level of protection as their more seasoned colleagues. Thirty-three senators were up for re-election. Because all three of the senatorial relatives who were killed were related to senators who were facing voters in November, those thirty-three families were given extra protection. But the other sixty-seven senators also demanded protection, even though their families were probably safe. While the policing agencies tried to prioritize protection levels on the basis of likely threat levels, it was the legislators who really made the decisions. And, like everything else in Congress, the decisions favored those with seniority.

All of the incumbents submitted family lists, which were constantly being amended upward as worried distant relatives made their presence known. Even with the lists and Congress' loose hand with taxpayers' dollars, the number of potential targets was in the tens of thousands, so protecting every target was virtually impossible. And frankly, the killer's point was as well made with a distant relative as it was with an immediate family member. So long as an incumbent's name was on the ballot, his or her relatives remained vulnerable.

The administration and Congress considered simply having everyone falsely say they would not seek re-election. If they did that, what could the killer do? However, it was August of an election year. Neither the Republicans nor the Democrats were willing to risk giving up a single seat. And, to make matters worse, non-incumbent candidates were carefully using some of the Congressional Killer's points to their advantage. They would say things like, "While we of course do condemn this man's actions, he is not the first to point out the ineffectiveness of the current Congress..." And some in the media were also getting on the bandwagon. Study after study was being discussed, showing things like how congressional benefits had swollen in recent years while living standards for the vast majority of Americans had been stagnant or declined. The ongoing failure to even discuss new gun control legislation after the Ken B. Anneywon gun sale fiasco was further enraging the public. "Not Anneywon" bumper stickers and tee shirts were becoming publicly acceptable ways of saying it was time for gun control legislation. Additionally, term limits and the process for implementing them were becoming a frequent topic of public debate.

Still, not a single congressman, congresswoman or senator declared that he or she would not seek re-election since the killer's letter was published. Not one. Several legislators wanted to, in response to demands of their family members, but the leaders of both parties were painting it as cowardly to even consider not seeking re-election.

Wherever possible, incumbents were encouraged to engage private security teams to protect their families, as a supplement to the federal efforts. The protection for the Gallagher family was a good example. The senator had hired a firm to protect each of her children and their families. The Feds let those groups provide or augment the front line protection and, in some cases, had their agents step back to watch, trying to catch the killer watching.

When he was in a Starbucks in St. Louis, there were two FBI

agents there as well. They were notified as Gallagher was about to leave the building and they watched the people sitting by Starbucks' window. They actually watched the killer look up. But his focus didn't seem to be on the senator's son. After only glancing in Gallagher's direction, his gaze appeared to follow an attractive young woman. After she passed, he looked down at the paper he was reading and didn't look up again for some time.

Chapter 60

The next morning, it was official. The bondholders had met and they declared Reynolds' holding company in default. They were suing to seize the assets of the Reynolds Ocean City Casino, Resort and Convention Center. A spokesman for the group made it clear that they wanted Reynolds out.

Hopper was devastated. Without the work in process payments from the Reynolds organization, he wouldn't be able to make the September rent payment on the space he leased for the casino job. He wasn't sure he could even make the next payroll payment, which was scheduled for the following Wednesday. As it turned out, even if he had the money, he wasn't allowed to pay his employees. When the banks and fabric companies that lent him the money he used to purchase the fabric and lease the space heard of the bondholders' attempt to seize Reynolds Ocean City's assets, they sued for an immediate freeze of Hopper Upholstery's assets. Three days after his mother first called him, he told his team to go home. He explained that he wasn't allowed to pay them, at least temporarily, because the company's assets were frozen. As a consequence, he didn't think it would be fair for them to work, even on jobs not pertaining to the Reynolds project. There were even two employees who had worked for his father, twenty-four years earlier. Everyone left, leaving Greg alone with Sarah and his mom.

Sarah had watched as Greg explained everything to his employees. In spite of the situation, she admired the way he handled everything. He was honest and open. He told people who depended on him, some for over twenty years, that they couldn't count on him anymore. Hopper Upholstery was finished. She could see that he was crushed. But as soon as they were alone, she had to ask him the most important question.

"What does it mean for us?"

"I'm not sure. We took out the second mortgage on the house.

If we don't make those payments, they will take it from us. But we can make those payments. I guess I'll try to find another job."

"Another job? What will you do?"

"I don't know. Maybe, for a while at least, I can get a job as an upholsterer. Between that and your salary, we should be able to hold on."

"What about Jane's tuition. It's due on the 21st. With room and board it's about $31,000. Do we have it?"

His shoulders slumped. "No."

"How much do we have?"

"About $23,000. I was supposed to get a progress payment from Reynolds next week. It was to be a $107,000 payment, Sarah. Our share would have easily covered the balance of the tuition. How could I have known?"

Chapter 61

After he decided not to kill Gallagher, he made his way slowly to the Pacific Northwest. His next target was in Medford, Oregon.

Wildfires were raging in many of the western states and he found work helping to fight the fires in Colorado. He wasn't a skilled firefighter, but he was strong and fit and a hard worker and was welcomed on one of the many support crews. It was a great hiding place for him. He slept in a tent camp and took his meals with the other workers. He disappeared for several weeks.

Chapter 62

The bankruptcy process seemed totally unfair. While Reynolds' assets beyond the Ocean City holding company were untouchable, Hopper's assets were seized. His mother and mother-in-law gave them the additional money they needed to pay Jane's tuition for her first semester at Middlebury. He and Sarah felt her education was more important than anything else, so they decided to pay the bill and see what happened.

Greg was so frustrated with his situation that he decided to go to Washington to see his congressman, Alan Taylor, and the senior senator from New York, Adam Keating. Taylor seemed sympathetic. Hopper explained that he and his father had owned and operated a small business on Long Island for over thirty-five years. They provided thirty-seven hard-working men and women with their livelihoods. Without Hopper Upholstery, many of them would be unable to find work. Two were in their early sixties.

At a time when the federal government was giving billions and billions of taxpayer dollars to companies like Citibank and AIG, couldn't they help a small company? He literally pleaded with him. The congressman responded with platitudes.

Next he found his way to Senator Keating's office. The attractive young staffer who manned the reception desk in Keating's office told him that the senator was a very busy man and that he couldn't see him. Greg said he would wait on the off chance that the senator could give him a few minutes. He waited during office hours for two days.

On the second day Reggie Reynolds himself walked into the office. Hopper had never met Reynolds, but like everyone else in America, he recognized him. Reynolds and his minions made his way to the receptionist's desk.

The receptionist, the same one who told Greg how busy the senator was, stood and greeted him. "Hi, Mr. Reynolds. It is so nice to see you again, sir."

"It's nice to see you, too." He didn't bother to call her by her name, Brenda, even though it was spelled out on a nameplate on her desk right in front of him.

She got a concerned look on her face. "We don't have you on the books, Mr. Reynolds. Have we messed up the schedule?"

"No, no. I was just in the area and wanted to talk to Adam for a bit. Can he see me?"

"Of course, Mr. Reynolds." Without even considering Greg she added, "The senator always has time for his constituents."

Then as if on cue, the door to the senator's office door opened and out walked Adam himself. The two men shook hands and semi-embraced and Keating led Reynolds into his office. He came out seventy minutes later.

Brenda started to escort Reynolds out of the office. As they were about to pass, Hopper stood and introduced himself. Reynolds was used to people fawning over him and wanting to shake his hand, so he paused for Hopper.

Greg extended his hand. "Mr. Reynolds, I'm Greg Hopper, from Hopper Upholstery. We're doing, well we were doing, the upholstering for the Reynolds Ocean City deal." He paused, expecting something back, but Reynolds quickly assessed the situation and resumed his exit. Greg blocked him, passively standing in his way, but blocking him nonetheless.

"Because of your firm's bankruptcy we've had to declare bankruptcy. All of my employees are out of work. We did nothing wrong, Mr. Reynolds. I was wondering if you could help us?"

"Look Mr. …"

"Hopper."

"Okay. Mr. Hopper. I don't know anything about your company. This stuff is all done through proper channels, legal channels."

"I mortgaged everything for this deal. I bought fabric for 7,400 chairs and for 1,200 couches. People have lost their jobs. Couldn't you use the fabric somewhere else?"

At that point, two capital policemen stepped into the reception room. Hopper looked from the officers to the receptionist. She had obviously called them.

The officers stood between Reynolds and Hopper, facing Hopper and seemingly protecting Reynolds. One asked, "Is there a problem here?"

"No. I just need to talk to Mr. Reynolds and Senator Keating. I was hoping they could help me."

The officer's face softened. Just looking at the situation, he knew Hopper probably hadn't done anything wrong and that Reynolds probably had. He also knew that the poor guy had already lost.

Keating stepped back out into the reception room and went to his constituent, at least to his wealthy constituent. "Is everything alright, Reggie?" Reynolds just nodded and left.

Keating turned back and faced Hopper and the two police officers. Before Keating could get away, Greg extended his hand. "Senator Keating, I'm Greg Hopper, from Garden City. I've been waiting two days to see you, sir."

Keating looked from Hopper to the two officers. Both were clearly sympathetic to the little guy. The senator stopped and spread his feet. Any audience that Hopper was allowed was apparently going to be in the reception area. "Thank you, sir. Here is the situation…"

In about two minutes, Greg outlined what had happened and explained that there were now thirty-eight New York taxpayers who were out of work.

Keating was only half listening. This guy had tried to play with the big boys and failed. It was that simple. "Mr. Hooper…"

"Hopper."

"Um, yes, Mr. Hopper." There was something familiar about his name. "I'm sorry, there is really nothing I can do. You took a chance and it didn't work out. I'm not sure what you think I can do for you."

"We didn't do anything wrong. We took a job, bought the materials to do the job, did a portion of the work. We were on schedule, ahead of schedule. And now he can just walk away and not pay us? How can that be? He has bankrupted my company and put all of these people out of work. I am going to lose my house. My daughter is a freshman in college…"

Keating cut him off. "Mr. Hopper, there is nothing I can do. The bankruptcy courts will sort everything out."

"Why can't you help?"

"We are not in the business of getting companies out of trouble. It sounds like you made a decision to expand your business and it didn't work out. It's that simple. Now I really have to get back to work."

"What about Citibank, AIG, GM, Chrysler? You bailed them out."

The senator's patience was at an end. One of his staffers approached to help extricate him, but before he did the senator looked at Hopper as if he simply didn't understand. "Sometimes we have to act for the greater good, Mr. Hopper. That is what we did in those instances." With that he turned his back and walked away.

Chapter 63

More than a week passed since the Arizona murder. The best available photographs and videos of the killer were posted and broadcast on every possible medium for most of that time and the Feds still didn't know the killer's identity.

They were using facial recognition technology to try to find his face among the millions and millions of video files they had access to every day. They were monitoring as many public venues as possible and running those faces against what they had on the killer. The problem was that they didn't have enough comparison points for the killer. In a perfect environment, facial recognition technology uses an algorithm to analyze the relative position, size and shape of the eyes, nose, cheekbones and jaw. Those characteristics are then used to search for other images with matching characteristics. Computers can search millions and millions of images and identify those with matching characteristics, matching numbers. But they didn't have enough consistent facial reference points on the killer. He always wore glasses, usually dark ones, and wore hats, wigs and facial hair to mask his underlying facial features. They had images of him at his motel in Missoula, in the parking garage in Florida and at the gun shop in Arizona. The technicians worked with the best images from those videos and came up with what they thought was their best guess as to his facial characteristics, but they simply didn't have enough consistent data. Every time they ran a comparison analysis, they came up with millions of matches, far too many to be useful.

They were also trying to figure out how he was traveling. They suspected he had a car and were running plate numbers from traffic or parking tickets, hotel registrations and toll plazas wherever they could. While that generated a number of leads, plate numbers that appeared around or near more than one of the kill sites, none panned out. Additionally they were checking car rental records, looking for correlations in rental dates, locations and names. Again, that analysis produced thousands of leads, but to date, none had been productive.

Chapter 64

After a few weeks of fighting fires, he was more relaxed than he had been in months. While the work was hard and the conditions were tough, it was generally only the experienced firefighters who were in truly dangerous situations. Most of the time he was digging trenches or providing support. But even at the times when the fire was close, he felt no fear. He knew he wouldn't survive much longer and he viewed his death as an end to the constant pressure he felt.

The team-oriented, exhausting work also kept him away from the news and from the anger he'd felt for so long. He considered staying, just stopping the killing and trying to meld into this group, but he knew that was impossible. So after eight days, when the group he was working with disbanded, he simply moved on. This was his third group and some of the other guys were talking about driving down to the southwestern part of the state to join the teams fighting the fires there, but he had to get back on track.

He sold his SUV and purchased another, an old black Nissan Pathfinder, and drove to Oregon. His target was a fifty-two year old male, the brother of a long-serving congressman from Portland who lived outside of Medford, in the southern part of the state.

Chapter 65

Greg's wife, Sarah, decided she would do anything she could to help. Her father, who left her and her mother when Sarah was just eight, had reached out to her a few times in recent years. To date Sarah had ignored his overtures, both out of loyalty to her mother and because she too had been devastated by his abandonment of them. She didn't learn until years later that he left her mother for another woman, whom he eventually married and with whom he started and raised a second family. Sarah had a half sister and half brother she'd never met.

Her father's new wife, Vivian Jackson, had been a teacher at the same school where he worked. She was a go-getter and a natural leader and rose within the ranks of the United Federation of Teachers and eventually became a congresswoman representing her home district in Brooklyn. She was in her fourth term.

Sarah took out one of her father's letters and using the address on the envelope, found his phone number and called him. A male voice answered the phone.

"Phil Jennings, please."

"May I ask who's calling?"

She paused and considered hanging up. "Sarah Hopper."

The man on the phone paused. It was clear he knew who she was. After a moment, he responded in a kind tone. "One second please. I'll get him."

She heard the sound of the phone being put down and then, "Dad." She almost hung up again as she waited.

"Hello. Sarah? Is it you?" His voice was instantly familiar, even after all these years. Tears welled in her eyes. She didn't know what to say next.

He filled the void. "Is it really you? I'm so glad you called, so glad to hear from you."

Her emotions were so mixed. For years, decades now, she had

hated him and missed him. She wanted him back. Yet she knew if he turned up, she'd reject him. She never understood why he'd left her. Lots of her friends' parents had split up, but she was the only child she knew of who had been totally abandoned by her father. She hated him because she blamed herself, feeling that she must have done something to drive him out.

"I need to talk to you. I need your help."

He couldn't believe she was talking to him. Over the years, he'd sometimes watched her, always from a distance, careful not to let her see him. He couldn't be that cruel. He already had been.

His voice was soft. "What do you need?"

"My husband's business is in trouble." She paused. "I'm married and have an eighteen year old daughter."

"I know."

She didn't respond to that. She had wondered if he knew anything about her, if he cared at all. "My husband, his name is Greg, he took over his father's upholstery business twenty-some years ago, when his father died. Last year, he got his biggest job ever, to upholster some of the furniture, a lot of it, for the Reynolds Ocean City Casino. He, we sunk everything we have into it. And now Reynolds is defaulting and simply walking away from the project. Everything we have invested will be lost. The government seems to be helping him, but they are screwing us. We can't even pay the people who worked for us on the project. The courts have frozen our assets."

She paused, unsure of whether he cared to help or even really listen to her.

"What do you want me to do, Sarah?" His tone was genuine, not at all sarcastic or skeptical.

"I'm not sure. I thought maybe your wife could help, that she could pull some strings."

Without pausing he responded, "Let me talk to her about it."

It was easier for them to talk about her situation than to really talk, about their own lives or the inevitable questions that she would eventually have to ask. They spent another fifteen minutes discussing the specifics of what had happened, including Greg's visit to the Hill. They left it that he would talk to his wife and get back to her.

When Sarah hung up she didn't know how to feel. It had been thirty-four years since they last spoke. Thirty-four years.

Chapter 66

Neil McCarthy was hoping that the killer would come after him. He knew his brother was too self-centered to ever step down and had heard him giving speeches on how he refused to bow to terrorists. He was full of shit. The truth was, the only person his congressman brother had ever cared about was himself. McCarthy sort of agreed with a lot of what the Congressional Killer said, but killing innocent people wasn't the way to fix the system. If the killer was murdering the politicians rather than their relatives, then McCarthy might even help him.

But he hoped the killer would come. He would take him out himself. His property was about fifteen miles northeast of Medford, Oregon, in the middle of nowhere. While they rarely spoke, his brother put him on a list of people who needed protection. McCarthy refused the protection, but had the feeling he was being watched. He assumed it was a protection unit and not the killer himself.

Chapter 67

Greg was able to find a job as an upholsterer for one of his larger competitors, A&H Upholsterers. The work kept him busy and provided him with some income, but not enough to keep making Jane's tuition payments at Middlebury.

He and Sarah considered selling their house, but the local real estate market was still so soft that even if they could find a buyer, they wouldn't clear enough to cover their two mortgages. Many people were in similar situations and the Hoppers read about people simply not paying their mortgages and staying in their homes until they were evicted. In the Hoppers' case, eviction seemed inevitable. Without the Reynolds job, they didn't think they could earn enough to make the payments on the second mortgage. But they both felt a moral obligation to continue to pay as much as they could, so until they were pushed out, they would do just that. They managed to remain current on the first mortgage, but were quickly getting further and further behind on the second.

They sought every financing option available for Jane's tuition. But again, with the dismal economy and massive defaults on student loans nationwide, new loans were very difficult to obtain, especially with the Hoppers' rapidly declining credit rating. Everything was falling apart.

Jane was aware that to pay for her first year at Middlebury her parents had borrowed everything they could, mostly from family members. Even with that, they had barely been able to make the payments. Consequently, she decided to transfer to Hofstra University on Long Island for her sophomore year. Jane was accepted into the honors program and was able to obtain a partial academic scholarship, so her tuition at Hofstra was about half that of Middlebury and the campus was close enough to home that she could live there and save the cost of room and board. Sarah and Greg had initially tried to talk her out of transferring, but ironically, she convinced them that it was the right thing to do.

Chapter 68

Agent Ready's approach to the case became both offensive and defensive. Defensively, along with the Secret Service and local law enforcement groups, the FBI was trying to protect as many congressional relatives as they could. Offensively, they were trying to find viable leads and follow up on every one.

Aside from video footage, the killer had been too clever and cautious to leave any other real evidence. So Agent Ready's primary tactic was to use the facial recognition technology to come up with faces and where possible with names to go with those faces. They focused a large portion of their efforts on places around known kill sites. For example, in Summerset and Ridge, Connecticut, where Evelyn Thompson was killed, they scanned faces at train and bus stations, airports, tollbooths, gas stations, ATMs and any closed circuit network they could access in the area, looking at time periods of up to four days before and after the day of the murder. In Connecticut and elsewhere, they sorted for images that corresponded to the facial characteristics they had from the Missoula, Panama City and Arizona videos and came up with thousands of faces. When possible, they matched those faces to names and ran computer checks on those names, looking for both criminal records and cross-checks with congressional correspondence. That still left them with thousands of leads. They further sorted those leads, trying to eliminate names as effectively as possible, first at the computer level, then through phone calls and finally through face-to-face meetings or surveillance.

One easy screening method was checking employment records. The killer travelled so consistently that it seemed unlikely he had a steady job. If he did, at the very least it was a job that allowed him considerable freedom. While millions of people worked off site but online, millions more still went to a plant or office or store to work each day. Simple checks of attendance records could efficiently eliminate thousands of potential suspects, once the Feds knew where the person worked.

In the same way that employer fingerprint records from places like banks, schools, hospitals and government contractors had long provided law enforcement agencies with data on individuals, digital identification photos now did so as well. Images that matched on facial points with the Montana, Florida and Arizona video images were sorted and scanned through employment databases. When matches were found, agents would call the employer and attempt to confirm the employee's whereabouts on days of and around the eight known killings. Thousands of potential suspects were eliminated in that way. For employees who travelled constantly or worked remotely, the individual's digital footprint could be checked and his whereabouts could be confirmed and checked against the killing dates and again, that person could be removed from the list of potential suspects.

Even with those methods of weeding out or eliminating potential suspects, Ready was left with thousands more to investigate. Most were unlikely, but he couldn't afford to ignore any potential lead.

Chapter 69

Initially the adjustment from Middlebury to Hofstra was difficult for Jane, especially academically. While Hofstra was a good school, average students there didn't have the same drive to learn, understand and think on their own as their Middlebury counterparts. Still Jane worked hard and came to find that the best students at Hofstra were as good as those at Middlebury. She applied herself and developed a reputation as a strong student and naturally gravitated to other strong students. Those students and the professors engaged her and she again found herself intellectually challenged and she started to thrive. Socially, she loved the kids at Hofstra. At Middlebury, while her good looks and kind personality helped her to fit in, she still felt like somewhat of an outsider. Many of the Middlebury students came from prep schools or from great wealth. They were nice, but different. The kids at Hofstra were more like Jane. So while she knew in her heart that she might be better off with a degree from Middlebury, that her degree would be perceived as more prestigious, she wasn't entirely sure that she would have gotten a better education there. Socially, she was happier at Hofstra.

For the first semester, she lived at home and commuted every day. But her dad found steady work and with his earnings and her mom's teaching salary, her parents insisted that she move out so that she could at least have a real college experience.

She eventually agreed and moved in with two other girls. The three women shared a small three bedroom, off-campus apartment about a mile from school. One roommate, Jen Defasio, was one of her closest friends in high school. While Jen was a good person and felt sorry that Jane had to transfer from Middlebury, she was thrilled to have her at Hofstra and insisted that she move in with her and her roommate when their lease expired. Jen's roommate, Erica, was a nursing student at Nassau University. Since she had odd hours, the three girls found an apartment near the Medical Center, to make it easier for Erica to get home after late shifts. The apartment was a bit of a hike from the Hofstra campus and sort of a pain for Jane and Jen, but it was affordable and there was frequent public bus service along Hempstead Turnpike, which ran between the two campuses.

Chapter 70

In light of the security he had seen in Kirkwood, he felt that scoping out McCarthy's place in the Oregon woods outside of Medford might be difficult. The congressman's brother's place was totally secluded. If there were protective guards nearby, at the very least his presence in the vicinity of the property would be likely to give the Feds another picture of him. They already had videos of him in the parking garage in Panama City, at the gun shop in Arizona and checking into his hotel in Missoula. While he was taking precautions to confuse facial recognition screens, he didn't want to risk giving the Feds' computers another potentially positive hit for a simple scouting mission. He decided that the risk of being flagged near McCarthy's rural property was simply too great. The congressman's brother was safe.

Chapter 71

Ready and his superiors had a tough decision to make with regard to how to handle and use the media. As always, there was tremendous pressure to release any information available about the killer. The pictures of him in the parking garage under Mrs. Sinclair's apartment building and the picture in the hotel lobby in Missoula had been widely distributed. But those pictures were really of little help. They showed two very different looking men and simply led to heightened expectations of a quick capture and to literally thousands of seemingly false leads. The Arizona video was even less helpful. For the most part, it only showed the top of his head under a baseball cap.

The Feds knew they were dealing with an intelligent, meticulous killer. He was using the media to convey his message and to create fear. Ready felt that the FBI could also use the media, to make the security measures they were using to protect congressional relatives seem far more extensive than they actually were. They implied that for relatives living in rural areas, they were using infrared surveillance to monitor nearby woods, mountainous or otherwise uninhabited areas. They even gave one network news crew an inside look at what they were doing, hoping the killer would see the broadcast and be deterred. The agent who gave the interview said the security teams were using the infrared surveillance to identify anyone approaching the homes of people they were protecting. If someone or something was in or even nearing a protected area, teams of agents or security personnel were sent to investigate. The interviewer asked if they were offering the protection to all congressional relatives and the agent responded, "To as many as possible."

Ready and his superiors knew that the killer staked out his victims and sometimes targeted people who lived in homes bordering uninhabited areas that offered cover, especially wooded areas as had been the case in several murders, including those of Mrs. Thompson in Connecticut and Dr. Morton in South Carolina. He hoped that the killer would see the interview and have second thoughts about scouting those easy-to-watch targets. They had the agent say that in more populated areas, they were also using the technology to identify people who seemed to be loitering in an area surrounding a congressional family member's home or work place. In areas around apartment buildings or offices, they were photographing and approaching people who seemed to be hanging around, potentially observing for prolonged periods, people who might be staking out a site.

The reality was that they were only using these measures to protect a fraction of the potentially targeted relatives, but even if the killer knew that, he wouldn't know who was being protected and who was not.

Chapter 72

One Thursday night in February of her sophomore year, just six weeks after she moved in with Jen and Erica, Jane went to a party near the Hofstra campus. She went with Jen, but met a boy she was sort of seeing at the party and stayed long after Jen left. In fact, she ended up staying until about 2:45.

Jane and the boy, Conor Donovan, met during Jane's first semester at Hofstra. While both had been attracted to each other, Conor was dating another girl. Between that and the fact that Jane still lived at home, their interaction never amounted to much more than innocent flirting. Conor and his old girlfriend broke up over the holidays and he and Jane had been casually seeing each other ever since. At first they had just sought each other out at parties, but for the past couple of weeks they were eating some meals together and were coordinating parts of their weekend plans.

The party on that Thursday was at Conor's apartment. While Conor and his roommates "cleaned up" for the party, the place was still foul. In warmer weather, college boys at Hofstra could count on rooftops or small backyards to avoid having to really clean up. But in the winter months, when they had to be inside, there was no getting around it. They made the place look what they considered to be presentable and then crammed fifty or sixty kids into a space that could comfortably handle about twenty-five. The forced proximity helped to camouflage the underlying mess during the party, but contributed to the ever building disgustingness of the apartment.

In spite of the surroundings, Jane and Conor and the other students were thoroughly enjoying themselves. By 1:30, which was about when Jen left, the crowd was starting to thin. By 2:00 it was just Jane, Conor and his three roommates and their girlfriends. While Jane and Conor felt they had the potential for a relationship, she wasn't even considering going to his room with him, let alone staying the night. Conor might have had other hopes, but he knew Jane was special and that he wanted to be with her, at whatever pace she was comfortable with. So as the others headed back to their bedrooms, they sat and talked.

At about 2:45, he offered to take her home. They considered ordering a cab, but that was expensive and at that late hour could take a while. So they decided to walk out to Fulton Avenue, which was a busy street. From there they could either walk, or, if they felt like it, catch a bus to within a block of Jane's apartment. It was a nice night and in spite of the late hour, there was still a fair amount of activity, so they decided to walk, at least to start.

Fulton Avenue is a four-lane street with a combination of commercial and residential buildings along either side. The commercial buildings include convenience stores, banks, gas stations, auto repair shops, used car dealerships, bars and dark, dingy looking, old school lounges. The residential areas comprise one to three story, low-income apartment buildings and complexes. Jane would have never walked along the street at that time of night by herself, but she felt safe with Conor. While the street was hardly busy with pedestrians, there were others out walking and partying.

As they were walking along the north side of Fulton, just west of the university, Conor saw a group of men walking towards them, about half a block away. The men didn't appear to be at all focused on Jane and Conor, but he thought it would be better not to pass them directly. He gently tugged Jane's hand, which he was holding, and started to cross the street. Before they could even step off the curb, they had to wait for three or four westbound cars, coming towards them along Fulton. By the time they were able to start to cross, the men were within fifteen feet of them, but still just talking among themselves. Conor felt as though things would be fine, that the guys would probably let them pass, but he didn't want to draw their attention by changing his course, so he and Jane waited for the last car to pass. Just as it did, his attention was drawn to a black SUV, which suddenly accelerated towards them from the eastbound lane across the street. The SUV's windshield was darkly tinted, but the two windows on the driver's side were both lowered. He saw gun barrels poking from the open windows. The approaching men, who also heard the car accelerate, scattered, diving in all directions. Before Conor could react, he saw the gun barrels flash repeatedly and heard the staccato sound of automatic weapons firing. He saw three barrels, two sticking out of the back window and one from the driver's window.

The SUV never paused. As it flew by, the people inside kept shooting at Conor and Jane and the men behind them. He heard more shots, coming from his side of the street, from near his feet and from behind him. Then he felt Jane tug at his arm. It all happened so quickly. He thought she was pulling him to get out of the way, but when he looked he saw she was falling to the ground. He got down, on top of her, trying to cover her.

The car passed. The men on the sidewalk behind and beside them kept firing in its direction. After it was well passed, they stood, all but one. Conor stood too, trying to pull Jane up with him. She moaned and felt like dead weight.

He looked from her to the men around them. They were staring at her and at their friend, who wasn't moving at all. He appeared to be dead. One of the men, a black guy who was about 6'2" knelt and shook him. The man didn't move.

"Fuck, he's dead."

Another said, "I'm hit too, in my side." He opened his coat and his shirt was covered in blood, on his left side, just above his hip.

Conor bent to Jane. "Jane, Jane. Are you okay?"

She didn't respond. Her eyes were open, focused on Conor, but she didn't respond. She didn't even try. All of the men stood there for a few seconds, staring at her and at Conor. There were five of them, six including the dead guy.

"Call 911. Hurry. I think she must be hit too." Conor opened her thick, black, ribbed down parka. Her white blouse was covered in blood. There seemed to be two sources: one visible, at her neck, near her right collar bone and another lower just below her left breast, at least that's where the blood was coming from.

"Call 911. Please."

The five men stared at him. He saw sympathy in some eyes and cold calculation in others. Conor realized that rather than helping, these guys might actually kill him, and Jane too, if she was still alive. He crouched over her, protecting her body from them. They looked at each other and seemed to reach a silent conclusion.

Chapter 73

Between facial recognition hits and calls from concerned citizens, the Feds had thousands of leads to pursue. Fortunately, Ready and his extensive team were able to eliminate the vast majority relatively easily. With the killer's broad geographic range, electronic transactions and especially employment or travel records in cities and towns distant from the kill sites exonerated most. It was possible that the killer had an accomplice who was providing him with a safe electronic record, but Ready doubted that. He thought that they had one smart, angry, probably crazy man who was operating off the grid and under a variety of aliases. While the digital age did make police work easier in many ways, such as tracking credit card spending and employment records and schedules, it also provided cover for those who knew how to use it. The Obama administration and the attorney general had any number of judges who were willing to give agents as many subpoenas and search warrants as they needed to follow up on practically any lead. The feeling within the administration, law enforcement and with the public in general, albeit to a lesser degree, was that the killer needed to be found as soon as possible, by any means possible. Individual rights such as privacy were being trampled, but this was viewed by most as an exceptional situation. The need to find and stop the killer was perceived, again by most, as more important than the potentially dangerous precedent being set with regard to the government's ability to look into the lives of its citizens.

For people leaving electronic traces, the subpoenas were extremely useful. But it was possible for individuals who wanted to live off the grid to do so and still operate in the digital world. Tens of thousands of stores around the country sold Visa, MasterCard and American Express "gift cards". Anyone could walk into a store and pay $5 above face value for what was effectively an untraceable debit card. And people could buy cards in amounts up to $500 without raising any suspicion. For $505 in cash, anyone could have a card that allowed him or her to get a hotel room or buy a train, bus or even plane ticket using any name they wanted. Similarly, the digital age also allowed easy access to fake IDs. How many people in New York or California know what a Kansas driver's license looks like? And even if they had some idea, licenses change with date of issue, so few people confidently ever really know. Anyone with access to the internet, a printer and the ability to laminate a piece of paper could make credible identification.

So for a clever, careful individual, it was very easy to operate in public, but still under the radar. While big name stores like Walmart, Stop & Shop and Walgreens that sold the gift cards generally had video surveillance, many mom and pop stores that also carried the cards did not. The Feds had been able to trace the source of the Visa gift card the suspect used at his hotel in Missoula to a convenience store in North Platte, Nebraska, but there were no video records of the purchase. The clerk who had been on duty at the time had a vague recollection of a heavy-set, middle-aged man buying the card. He remembered because the man said he was buying it as a gift for his son who was getting married and going on his honeymoon. But the clerk couldn't give any sort of a specific description or confirm that he was the man in the widely circulated videos of the Congressional Killer.

Nonetheless most people operated with traceable electronic activity and with those records establishing credible alibis, the Feds were able to exonerate thousands of suspects. The hundreds of leads they couldn't exonerate required much more work. The names given in these cases were often people whom the callers knew but hadn't seen in some time. If they could give names and better still some idea of where the suspect worked or had worked, the Feds could get a social security number and pretty easily track the man down, as long as he was working and filing tax returns. But in the current economy, with about 7% officially unemployed and another 7% so discouraged that they weren't even seeking employment, there was a good chance that the killer was not employed and may not have been for sometime. Ready's experience had shown that idle men were more likely to get into trouble. Busy, engaged men were often, though far from always, more satisfied with their lives than men with too much time on their hands. The agent believed that the killer was either unemployed or self-employed. Still, leads were leads and even if employment information led them on a dated trail, it was at least a starting point.

All around the country there were literally hundreds of thousands of men who had lost their jobs and, sometimes, their homes and families or wives. Many of those men moved to different parts of the country to find work or just to get away from their old, more successful lives. Finding those men was often difficult.

Ready adopted a rating system, one often used within the Bureau, to always have a ranked, top 100 suspects. The higher the name was on the list, the more attention the individual was given and the quicker his name was removed, if he could be found. Many of the top names were simply missing. With the loss of their jobs, the men who tended to remain on the list had fallen off the grid. They had often been through hard times, especially financially, and had seen a serious deterioration in their credit ratings and in their ability to access credit at all. Many of those men were forced into a cash-only existence and were therefore largely off the traceable electronic system. If they remained unemployed or found under-the-table, part-time work, there was often no record of their activities. Tracking them down involved old fashioned police work: talking to family, friends and former work associates, looking for any hint of a trail and then following that trail. The Feds and local police forces burned through thousands of man-hours and millions of dollars tracking these men down. When they were finally found, if they were, they were often beaten, sad men. But so far, none were murderers.

Many of the names at the top of the list were stale. In some cases, no new information had been found in weeks. And in most cases, potential motives were impossible to determine. Life itself may have made the suspects bitter enough to kill or their unemployment or the degradation of their lifestyles could be sufficient cause in a damaged mind. But to hone the list, Ready and his fellow agents learned what they could about the men, to try to find real motive.

One name caught his agents' attention: Greg Hopper.

Chapter 74

While they were still struggling financially, Greg and Sarah had been able to hold onto their house. Greg was working fulltime for his former competitor and making decent money. With that and Sarah's income from teaching and extra money she made tutoring young students, they had been able to get current on their second mortgage. They were also able to get financial aid from Hofstra to help make Jane's already significantly lower tuition payments.

Sarah knew that the loss of his business and Jane's forced transfer from Middlebury weighed heavily on her husband. He had never been an egotistical man, but he was quietly proud of the fact that he had been able to step into his father's shoes and take care of his family. While he never minded not having a degree himself, he wanted the best for his daughter and when she was accepted at Middlebury, it had been one of the happiest days of his life. Even though she regularly reassured him that Jane was happier at Hofstra and that in the honors program she was getting an education that rivaled the one she had been getting in Vermont, Sarah knew he blamed himself for everything. He felt that if he hadn't been so ambitious, if he had listened to her, they wouldn't be in the situation they were in.

She tried to tell him that their situation wasn't that bad, that they still had their home and that Jane was happy and close, but she could see a difference in him. For Greg, even though it had been forced on him, Hopper Upholstery had never been a job or a burden. It was a source of pride and challenge and joy. He had been able to support his family and to create jobs to help support other families. Now he had to drag himself to work every day. He tried to hide it and she was sure he worked very hard and was a great employee, but for the first time in his life, his work was a job.

In spite of all that, things were slowly getting back to normal. They were still careful with every dollar they spent, but recently they had started to see friends again and to go out for a movie and dinner. Sarah thought she was getting her husband back.

And then, late one night, the phone rang.

Chapter 75

He decided he had to change his approach. With the additional security surrounding congressional relatives, home kills were going to be difficult if not impossible. But he wanted to keep the pressure on. The election was nearing and incumbents were running nervously, largely out of fear, but not fear for their relatives' lives. They feared defeat at the polls.

Across the country, many non-incumbent candidates were following a carefully crafted script in order to attract disaffected voters. Their pitch was that the system was broken and that for well over two decades, since Clinton was elected in 1992, or maybe since Reagan's first term in 1980, partisanship had been growing and the demands on the newly elected to toe party lines had grown with every election and administration, no matter which party was in power. While many freshman senators and congressmen and congresswomen went in with good intentions, the extremists in each party called the shots and recent freshmen generally caved to the wishes of those in power. Some Tea Party Republicans tried to remain independent, but their efforts led to even more partisanship and ultimately stalemate. The only way to really affect change, the script went, was to bring in new men and women. The new candidates were careful to never say "new blood." They went on to say that the system itself needed changing. Always with the caveat that they of course obviously denounced and deplored the recent illegal and horrific actions, some candidates explicitly pledged that they would fight for term limits and, in some cases, would commit to not serve for more than six years. Finally but emphatically, they added that since they would only be serving for a short time, they could put the peoples' interest ahead of their own and would therefore not be beholden to special interest groups like the NRA. The candidates made it clear they favored bans on assault weapons and mega-round ammunition magazines and that there should of course be mandatory background checks for gun sales in stores, at gun shows and on the internet.

The shorter evening news clip pitch for would-be congressmen and senators was, "The system is broken and needs to be fixed. The incumbents have had their chance and we all know how well that has worked. I want to be part of the solution so I am pledging to serve for no more than six years and to fight for term limits. I will be beholden to no one and able to vote my conscience and to act and vote for the greater good."

His message was getting through. But he knew this election was his only chance. He had to figure out a way to make people really hate incumbents and to see them for the self-interested phonies they were.

Chapter 76

Conor remained bent over Jane, unsure whether they would shoot him or just leave. Thankfully, after taking their dead friend's gun and wallet, the five men left, running east on Fulton and then splitting up and disappearing onto side streets. He turned his attention back to Jane, trying to revive her. Her eyes were closed now, but she was still breathing.

In the distance, he heard sirens. Someone must have called the police. He called too, telling the 911 operator that his friend had been shot and that he needed an ambulance and that another man was lying nearby, dead. He told her the location and, after the operator established that the shooters were gone and that he was safe, she coached him on how to try to help Jane. He could still feel a pulse and she was breathing.

By the time the police arrived, just a couple of minutes later, there was a small crowd gathered around Conor and Jane and the dead man. After they checked Conor and Jane and the man's body for weapons, one officer questioned Conor while the other tried to help Jane. Conor explained what he had seen, describing the SUV, which he thought was a black Mercedes, and the men who were apparently the target of the attack. Other than to say that there were six of them, including the dead man, that they were black and in their early to mid twenties and that one of the survivors had been shot, he didn't give the police much to go on.

Within fifteen minutes, an ambulance had taken Jane away and there were over ten police and EMS vehicles on the scene. Conor wanted to go with Jane, but the police kept him for questioning. Another man, who was about half a block west of and across the street from Jane and Conor during the shooting, largely confirmed Conor's version of what transpired. He also confirmed that the shooters were driving a black Mercedes SUV and said that the car had new style New York plates starting with 9A. Police found an iPhone on the dead man and were able to identify him as James Simpson, a twenty-six year old from Jackson Heights in Queens. Simpson had served time for a drug related assault.

Chapter 77

At 4:15 am, Greg was startled awake by the bedside phone. He looked at his alarm clock and anxiously answered the phone, as any parent would at that hour.

"Hello."

"Is this Mr. Hopper?"

"Yes."

"Mr. Hopper, do you have a daughter named Jane?"

"Yes, yes. What's happened? Who is this?"

The voice on the other end hesitated. "Sir, I'm Officer Tim Wright, of the Nassau County Sheriff's Department. I'm afraid I have some bad news. Your daughter has been in what appears to be an accident."

"Is she alright? What happened?" Greg was standing now, putting on his pants as Sarah got up too, looking at him desperately, holding up her hands to ask: What happened?

Greg said to her, "Jane's been in an accident."

"Your daughter," the officer paused. "She's been shot."

"Shot? Jane? Is she alright?"

"She's at the Nassau University Medical Center, in the ER. I suggest you get there as quickly as possible, sir."

Greg gave the officer his cell phone number and told him that he and his wife were on their way.

"Is she alright?"

"I'm not sure, sir. I believe they have taken her into surgery. You should get to the hospital. The doctors and police there can give you more information."

Greg could hear a sense of urgency in the policeman's voice. He hung up and told Sarah everything the officer said as they threw on their clothes and raced for the car. The twenty-five minute drive was the longest of their lives. They turned on a local news station and heard a report of a shooting near Hofstra in which one man was killed and a woman was shot, apparently multiple times. She was in critical condition.

Chapter 78

After the failures in Medford and St. Louis, he decided to lay low for a while. He drove to the outskirts of Oakland and checked into a Knights Inn.

There he plotted his next move.

Chapter 79

Seven weeks after receiving his first letter from the Congressional Killer, Mike Williams of *The Erie Star* received what he assumed was his second.

> *Dear Mr. Williams,*
>
> *In spite of my actions and countless other equally terrible school and workplace shootings and carjackings and ever increasing numbers of gun related deaths in this country, Congress remains unwilling to act. Between 80 and 90% of Americans are in favor of gun control legislation, but Congress isn't even discussing it. Our elected officials are more interested in contributions from groups like the NRA than they are in serving their constituents and the greater good. They are literally choosing to put murder weapons in the hands of criminals. Enough is enough.*
>
> *I am giving Congress two weeks to enact legislation that bans assault weapons, prohibits the sale of ammunition magazines holding more than six rounds and that requires mandatory fifteen day waiting periods to enable legitimate background checks on all gun purchases. And finally, purchases of firearms or ammunition online or at gun shows should be banned, because guns purchased that way are too easily obtained.*
>
> *If Congress simply passes that legislation and President Obama signs it into law, I will turn myself in within twenty-fours hours. If not, I will expand my target population to include every constituent of every congressman, congresswoman and senator. So, if you don't pass the legislation, your families and your constituents will all be targets. The only people who will be safe will be you.*
>
> *By making this pledge, I am risking my primary cause, term limits. I am willing to do this for two reasons. First, because I believe that there is a movement afoot that will force term limits on elected officials, even after I am gone. Second, and I am stating*

this openly, I am so confident that in spite of the fact that the vast majority of Americans want gun control legislation, 80 to 90% of your voters, in spite of that overwhelming mandate, I am sure that you, the Congress, will not pass the legislation. Your greed and legislative incompetence and insensitivity are too great. Because you Republicans and Democrats and Tea Party members are so self interested, you will not be willing or able to pass the legislation your country desperately wants and needs. As a result, the people you have elected to serve will be so thoroughly disgusted by your actions that with or without me, they will vote overwhelmingly against incumbents in the next election, just four weeks from now.

To the voters, I also suggest that you demand that all candidates for the US Congress and Senate pledge not to serve more than six years. Terms in the House should be reset to six years with one third of the seats subject to election every two years, the same way it is done in the Senate. To keep candidates honest, have them sign documents stating that if they break the one-term pledge, they will forgo all of the ridiculous long-term health and pension benefits and access to funds contributed to leadership PACs that your elected officials and their predecessors have been able to legislate for themselves. While you are at it you might also mandate that Congress revises their benefit and pay packages. Have them offer three alternative health care plans in the election after this one and let the nation's voters decide what benefits and salaries their elected officials are entitled to. Give them choices of coverage similar to those offered to us. Finally, mandate that any future pay or benefit changes must be approved in national elections.

We are supposed to have a government of the people, by the people, for the people. Let's put the power back in the people's hands.

Williams read the letter three times. Then he called his boss and the FBI. The next day, for the third time in a few months, *The Erie Star* scooped the world.

Chapter 80

When Sarah and Greg arrived at Nassau University Medical Center they were met by police and immediately taken to a waiting room where they were briefed, first by a doctor.

Jane was in surgery. She had been shot three times, twice in the chest and once in the back of her head. While the chest wounds were serious, the doctors felt they could be managed. At this point, they weren't sure about the head wound. She was apparently semi-conscious immediately after the shooting, but quickly lost consciousness and had not regained it.

Sarah fired out a series of questions. Greg just listened.

After the doctor finished his briefing and answered as many of Sarah's questions as he could, a police lieutenant explained what they thought had happened.

Apparently at about 3 am, Jane and a friend, Conor Donovan, were walking from his apartment, which was just west of the Hofstra campus, to Jane's place. They had been at a party at the young man's house. Jane and Conor were heading east on Fulton Street. Six men, all in their twenties, were walking towards them. According to Conor and another witness, just as the men were approaching Conor and Jane, a black SUV accelerated towards them from the west, from behind them. The occupants of the SUV opened fire on the approaching men. The other witness said that some of the men returned fire. Conor and Jane were caught in the crossfire. Jane was hit three times. The officers weren't entirely sure at this point but they felt that two of the shots that hit Jane came from the SUV and one came from the men returning fire.

One of the six men was killed and Conor was sure that at least one of the other five was also hit. The officer added that a witness said that as soon as the shooting started, Conor threw his body over Jane, trying to protect her.

Two hours later Greg and Sarah were told that their daughter was dead.

Chapter 81

Ready frequently reviewed the files of the top fifty suspects. Many of those files were stagnant because there were no recent traces of the suspects. The seventeenth name on the list was Greg Hopper. Hopper had been through a lot in the past few years.

Like many other people on the suspect list, the Feds first heard about Hopper from tips phoned into the hotline when the Florida and Missoula pictures were initially released. Three different people called in saying that the images looked like Hopper. Three wasn't a big number. Over thirty people in a small town in Oklahoma called in about one unfortunate lookalike, a guy named Jeff Greisch. Greisch hadn't been more than a hundred miles from his hometown of Lawton in over six months and had ironclad alibis. He had been at work or at home or in places with witnesses on the days of the killings, so the FBI quickly cleared him. But people in his town still suspected the poor guy.

Originally, the FBI agent assigned to look into Hopper tried to check his employment records, but he hadn't worked in over a year or, perhaps more accurately, he hadn't reported any income during that time. His wife was a teacher and they had always filed jointly, until the last filing year when she filed a separate return and he didn't file at all.

Lots of people were unemployed in the current economic environment. But the Feds were looking for someone who had become disenfranchised and angry. Hopper looked like a potential suspect.

His name was initially moved from the broadest list of names, from which most suspects were cleared, to a still very long list that required more attention. At this level, rather than just checking computer records, phone calls were made. Agent George Benitez was assigned to look into Hopper, along with dozens of other names. Benitez's first step was to call Hopper's last known employer, A&H Upholstery.

He called and asked to speak to the owner, a man named Harold Fryburg. Fryburg was a little suspicious of the call at first and not especially forthcoming with information. Benitez decided to drive out to Garden City to talk face to face.

When he appeared at his door and showed his credentials, as was often the case, the business owner opened right up. It turned out that Greg Hopper had been through the mill over the past few years. Fryburg told Benitez about Hopper as only a small town colleague could, describing details about every success and failure. By the time Fryburg got to Reggie Reynolds defaulting on the casino deal, Benitez was taking detailed notes.

Fryburg said he felt sorry for Hopper. So when he came to him looking for work as an upholsterer, he hired him. He said that it turned out to be a great hire. He was a skilled worker and had the sort of pride in his workmanship that only an owner does. He worked long hours at A&H and took other part-time jobs, doing whatever he could to hold onto his house and to pay for his daughter's college education.

Hopper's wife was a teacher so between Greg's income and hers, they worked their way out from under the pile of debt that he had taken on for the Reynolds Casino deal. Even with that, his daughter had been forced to transfer from some fancy private college in New England to Hofstra. But for a while, it looked as though things were going to be all right for Hopper and his family.

Benitez could tell Fryburg liked Hopper. But the elderly man seemed to visibly tire as he described what happened next. One night about eighteen months ago, Hopper's daughter Jane had been killed by crossfire in a drive-by shooting near Hofstra. It was some sort of a drug turf war or something. The boy she was with was okay, but Jane died that night.

Hopper hadn't been back to work since. Fryburg had gone to the funeral. He said it was awful, as was any funeral for someone that young, killed so senselessly.

Chapter 82

The public debate changed the day the second letter was published in *The Erie Star*. After the massacre at Sandy Hook Elementary School in Connecticut, the American public had been truly upset and expected that there would finally be action on gun control legislation at a national level. When the legislation failed, people were disgusted with Congress and disappointed in President Obama for his lack of real leadership on the issue, but they were used to politicians failing and the gun control issue receded to where the NRA liked it, on the back burner. However during the period since Sandy Hook, it seemed there had been a shooting of some sort almost every week.

News anchors, editorialists, pundits, bloggers and the man on the street were all debating the points raised by the Congressional Killer and most were agreeing with him. Prior gun control debate revolved around half measures like reverting to magazines with a maximum of fifteen rounds or a mandatory three-day waiting period. Conversely, the killer was setting the sort of standards dictated by common sense rather than compromise. Momentum was gathering for the legislation and against inaction. If that wasn't enough, the fact that if Congress did not pass the legislation, the killer would expand his target population to include everyone except congressmen and congresswomen and senators made people furious. If Congress simply wrote into law what polls now showed 91% of voters wanted, they could rid the country of a killer and help to solve a much bigger problem.

The pressure to pass gun control legislation was at fever pitch.

The media and the public also began to openly discuss the lavish benefits Congress had rewarded itself with over the past decades. A congressman or congresswoman who served one term, two years, was entitled to lifetime health care benefits. Lifetime. And this wasn't Obama Care. They had entitled themselves to first rate, choose your doctor, choose your hospital, choose your treatment benefits.

Paper after paper and news show after news show outlined the incredible pay and benefits packages the officials had awarded themselves. The idea of throwing them all out and starting with a fresh batch of limited term legislators was gaining popularity in the polls every day. As was the suggestion of forcing Congress to reset their benefits packages and laying those benefits out for the public to vote on, in the same way that the public chooses packages under the new universal healthcare plans at state levels. People also liked the idea of congressional pay raises being subject to popular vote, though most agreed that if that happened, it would be years before legislators saw an additional penny.

The consensus was that a great deal of what the killer demanded would be good for the country. Term limits solved a lot of problems. The short-term nature of service associated with term limits effectively gave all legislators equal power and enabled individual congressmen and congresswomen and senators to vote with their conscience instead of having to toe party lines to gain positions on more powerful committees. They could vote for the greater good without repercussions. With one six-year term they could also focus on legislation rather than re-election and fundraising. Consequently, they wouldn't be dependent on or beholden to lobbyists or campaign contributors because they wouldn't need their money to get re-elected. Term limits would also allow for changes in lobbying practices. Poll after poll showed that people believed that the vast majority of elected officials went to Washington intending to do the right things, but became jaded with years of service. The belief was that if you sent in a bunch of new men and women to serve one six-year term, whether in the House and Senate, with one third being replaced every two years, those legislators, most of them at least, would do what their constituents elected them to do, rather than bending to the will of lobbyists like the NRA. Term limits didn't immediately solve the problems created by the power of lobbyists or self-serving perks like leadership PACs, but they were a big step in the right direction. If honest, limited-term politicians were elected they could enact legislation that could affect needed change. The argument that America needed seasoned politicians to keep things running effectively had had its chance. An increasing number of citizens felt that by the time politicians became seasoned, they had made so many compromises and owed so many debts and were beholden to so many lobbyists, contributors and other politicians, that they could no longer vote objectively. There was real risk that Congress might lose some efficiency and some historical perspective because it lost its ultra-seasoned members, but that seemed a risk worth taking. The body had become so ineffective and so bogged down in partisanship that the benefits of change seemed likely to outweigh some real costs of limited terms. And truly effective legislators could still serve twelve years, six in the House and then, if they were good enough, another six in the Senate.

The more they were discussed, the more ground many of the killer's demands gained with the general public.

Chapter 83

After Jane died so did her parents' marriage.

Her funeral was brutal. Hundreds of kids from Jane's high school and from Hofstra and Middlebury made the trip. Their presence was welcome for Sarah and Greg, but at the same time painful. They were all so young, with their whole lives ahead of them.

For a few months after her death, the Hoppers tried to make things work. After about three weeks, Sarah went back to work. Greg never did. For a while, he just hung around the house. He thought about going to work, but he couldn't make himself do it. He just didn't care.

The police tracked down the group of men who were the targets when Jane was shot. With the dead man's identity, James Simpson, they were able to find his associates and the shooters from the SUV. They were awaiting trial.

The two shots that hit Jane in the chest were fired from the SUV with an AR-15, the most commonly sold assault rifle in the country. The gun lobby argued that it was a rifle, not an assault weapon, because unlike machine guns, which fired 850 to 1,000 rounds per minute, the AR-15 could only fire between 45 and 60 rounds per minute, depending on the skill of the operator. And again, unlike a truly automatic weapon, which could fire multiple rounds each time the trigger was pulled, the AR-15 could only fire one round with each trigger pull. The difference was irrelevant. Forty-five rounds per minute was beyond ridiculous. The AR-15 that wounded Jane had been purchased online. The buyer, who was also the shooter, was a convicted felon. He'd used a fictitious name to buy the assault rifle, but gave his real address.

The shot that actually killed Jane was fired from behind, from one of the six men. The five survivors were now trying to paint themselves as victims. They claimed that their deceased friend, James Simpson, fired the shot that hit and ultimately killed Jane. His gun was a Glock 19 with a seventeen round magazine. The pistol was purchased in South Carolina.

When he filled out the application for the pistol, Simpson, who served three years for assault, was able to fraudulently affirm that he was not a convicted felon by simply checking a box on the registration form for the gun permit.

Greg considered going after the thugs who killed Jane, but the police found them quickly and they were likely to be in prison for a long time. He also considered blaming the boy she was with, Conor Donovan. But an eyewitness testified that as soon as the shooting started, the boy threw his body over Jane, trying to protect her from the gunshots. While Hopper blamed Donovan for having his daughter out that late, he knew even that wasn't really the boy's fault. He was quietly seething and had to find some outlet for his anger.

Chapter 84

After his meeting with Hopper's former employer, Harold Fryburg, Agent Benitez reviewed his notes. Hopper's profile fit so many of the characteristics they were looking for in the killer. He emailed his report to Sean Ready, the agent heading the task force, and followed up with a call, encouraging Ready to look at it immediately.

Ready read the report and agreed that Hopper looked like a viable candidate. It had been weeks since the last killing and four days since *The Erie Star*'s report of the killer's new demands. It was hard enough trying to protect families of long-serving congressmen. If the two weeks elapsed without congressional action and the killer widened his target base to pretty much everyone except Congress, there was no hope for protection. Furthermore, the pressure from Congress and the top brass in the Bureau to find the killer before the two-week deadline expired was higher than ever. Ready literally had any resource he needed at his disposal.

He flew to New York to meet with Benitez and to put together a plan and a team to investigate Hopper.

When he landed at LaGuardia, Benitez met him at the airport and together they drove to Hopper's house in Garden City. He and Benitez considered setting up a meeting with Hopper's wife, but decided just to show up.

They got to her house at about 5:20 on a Wednesday afternoon. When they arrived, there were already two cars and four agents parked on her street, a few houses away. The agents said she got home at about 4:45, presumably from her job as a second grade teacher at a nearby grammar school, McArthur Elementary. Ready sent one of the surveillance cars to the street behind her house, to watch from there in the event anyone fled from Hopper's backyard.

He and Benitez parked right in front of her house, a modest but well maintained three-bedroom cape in a nice suburban neighborhood of similar homes. They walked up the Hoppers' driveway to the front walkway and to the front door. Mrs. Hopper apparently saw them coming and opened the door as they approached.

Ready was struck by how beautiful she was. He knew from Benitez's report that she was 44 years old. She was about 5'7" and weighed about 130. Wearing dress slacks and a fitted blouse, she was stunning, even after all she had been through.

"Can I help you?"

Ready and Benitez reached for their badges and showed them as Ready spoke. "Hello, Mrs. Hopper? Sarah Hopper?"

She didn't seem surprised to see officers at her door. Ready wondered if she was expecting them or if she thought they were there with regard to her daughter's murder.

"Yes. I'm Sarah Hopper."

"Mrs. Hopper, I'm Agent Sean Ready from the FBI. This is my associate, Agent George Benitez. We were wondering if we could talk to you?"

Sarah extended her hand to each man, something that wasn't all that common among people, especially women, being visited unexpectedly by FBI agents.

"Nice to meet you officers, or agents. Would you like to come in?" Her voice was neither overly friendly nor curt.

She led them into their family room, which was comfortable and nice. In spite of everything that had happened, it seemed like it was, or at least had been, a happy home. There were family pictures, mostly of Jane, but some of all of them, everywhere. The agents tried to get a good look at pictures of her husband as they were seated.

Once they were all sitting she turned to Agent Ready, "What can I do for you?"

"First of all, ma'am, I'd like to say how sorry I am for your loss."

"Thank you. Are you here about Jane? I didn't realize the FBI was involved in her case."

"No ma'am, we're not here about Jane. We're here to discuss your husband."

Her face immediately showed concern, fear. "Has something

happened? Is he okay?"

"As far as we know, ma'am, he's fine. We're trying to find him. Do you know where he is?"

"Why are you trying to find him? Has he done something wrong?"

"We're not sure, ma'am. We just want to talk to him."

"Why?"

Ready looked at Benitez and then back to Mrs. Hopper. "When was the last time you saw him?"

She kept her eyes on him. They were deep blue and clear and confident.

She looked tired and weary, but not at all beaten.

"I haven't seen Greg in over a year. I have heard from him a few times, but I haven't seen him."

Agents were already getting a subpoena for her phone records, but they didn't have them yet.

"May I ask why you haven't seen him? Do you know where he is?"

"What is this about?"

"If you could just answer a few more questions, Mrs. Hopper, I will explain everything."

She looked at him for a moment and then nodded.

"Where is your husband, Mrs. Hopper?"

"I don't know. As you apparently know, nineteen months ago our daughter was killed." She paused. Though she said it clearly, it was apparent it was still a very difficult thing for her to say or accept. "My husband changed that night. I lost him, too. I lost them both."

She looked down. Ready paused for a moment and when she looked back up at him he asked an open-ended question, trying to get whatever she would give him. "What happened?"

Sarah gathered her thoughts and looked from him to Agent Benitez. Even in this situation, she was unconsciously kind and polite, including both men in the discussion. "My family has been through a great deal in the past few years. Three years ago, we lost our business. My husband ran his family's upholstery business and he was doing a project for the Reynolds Casino in Ocean City. It was the biggest project we had ever done and we had to borrow a lot of money to do it. When Reynolds walked out on the deal and it went into receivership, my husband was forced to close his company and to lay off all of the people who worked for him. He tried to keep it open. He went to Washington and spoke to representatives there and I reached out to a congresswoman I know. No one helped."

Ready could hear disdain in her voice when she mentioned Reggie Reynolds and the people in Washington.

"That was very tough on us. Our daughter, Jane, she was a freshman at Middlebury College in Vermont when this all happened. After the company closed, we..." She paused and then continued. Her voice was a little weaker. "After the company closed, well, we couldn't afford Middebury's tuition. Almost immediately, Greg found another job, upholstering for another company and he did some retail work at night. With that and my income from teaching, I teach second grade here in town, we scraped by enough to keep her in for all of her freshman year. But without the income from Hopper Upholstery, we just couldn't do it." Her eyes teared slightly. "She transferred to Hofstra here on Long Island. With a partial scholarship she was awarded, the tuition was about half of what we were paying for Middlebury. It was her idea. She knew we couldn't afford Middlebury. For the first semester, she lived here with us. But in her second semester, we insisted she live near the campus. We wanted her to have a real college experience." She emphasized the word we. "Six weeks after she started there, on a Thursday night..."

At that point, she started to cry. She stood and went to the kitchen, an open room separated from the family room by a breakfast counter. She took a tissue from a box on the counter and wiped her eyes.

Ready and Benitez were quiet, standing when she stood but saying nothing. She came back into the room and nodded for them to sit. She remained standing.

"Greg was never the same after that. He blamed himself. Because of me, I think."

Ready looked at her, not understanding. She saw his confusion and went on. "I wasn't generally involved in the business, but because the Reynolds deal required that we take on so much additional debt, beyond our mortgage, Greg asked for my opinion. I never actually said no, but I wasn't really behind it. It just seemed too risky."

She paced as she spoke. Ready wasn't sure if she had ever told anyone all of this before.

"When the deal failed, we almost lost our house. But he worked so hard, so hard and for so many hours each week. Eventually we got current on our mortgages again." She paused then added, "With some help from our family, I thought we were going to be okay. It hurt him to lose his company. It had been his father's and Greg took it over when his dad died. He quit college and came home at the age of twenty and took over. He supported his mom and his sisters, helped put them through college. He grew the company. He was proud of it. He loved his dad and it was theirs."

She sat again. "When he had to let all those people go, his employees, I think he felt ashamed and stupid. But he worked hard and we got through it. And then…"

Ready didn't want to interrupt. She was opening and he didn't want to stop her, but he had to lead her, to keep her going. "I can't imagine, Mrs. Hopper."

She looked at him. He thought she was evaluating him. She gave him a sad smile, seeming to believe his sincerity.

"For a while after her death, for a few months, he was engaged, but not in a good way. He was focused on her killers and on the boy she was with the night she was killed. I was afraid he was going to do something."

She looked from Ready to Benitez, fully aware they were FBI agents, admitting that she feared what he might do. "He was so angry. He wanted someone to blame."

Ready asked, "Who did he blame?"

She paused again and considered the question. "In the end, I think only himself." Then she retracted that. "When they caught those gangs, I think he thought those men would be punished. And the Donovan boy, Conor, well he threw himself over Jane, trying to protect her from the bullets. The witness said he did it right away, almost as soon as the shots were fired.

"Greg is a very rational man. He was angry that the boy kept her out so late. But he knew she stayed out late with him. She was an independent young woman."

She started to cry openly. "Conor came to see us. He came with his parents. They were with him, but he spoke for himself. He faced us and answered all of our questions. That was so important to us, to know. Greg didn't blame him."

Ready paused for a moment then asked, "Who did he blame?"

"The gun that killed our daughter; it was a semi-automatic pistol, a Glock something. Greg became fixated on that, on all of the guns used in the shooting. The man who shot our daughter, James Simpson, was a convicted felon. He should have never been allowed to buy the gun, any gun. The gun laws are so lax, so ridiculously stupid that all he had to do was lie on an application form. He checked a box affirming he wasn't a convicted felon, and that was enough to clear him to get a gun, a semi-automatic murder weapon."

Ready paused again, absorbing what she said and considering his next question. "Did he blame the people who sold Simpson the gun?"

"No. They didn't break any laws. It was the laws themselves. Laws that let criminals buy guns. Laws that let billionaires walk away from their debts while average people have to pay off theirs."

"Who then?"

"It's as if the people making the laws don't care about what happens to average people. After all of the shootings over the years, before Jane's death, in places like Columbine and Aurora and Sandy Hook, they didn't do anything. After all those little kids were massacred in Connecticut, the whole country wanted gun control legislation. But, in spite of a bunch of bluster on television, in front of the cameras, Congress didn't do anything. When Greg learned that Simpson was a felon and that he was able to get a gun by just checking a box on an application form, he couldn't believe it. Maybe he would have gotten another gun somewhere else, but he legally purchased the gun that killed our daughter. A convicted criminal shouldn't be allowed to do that. Greg said Congress has had so many chances to help the American people and they never did anything about it. And they get on TV and brag and act as if they are doing good things for the country. It is all just lies. The gun companies and the NRA and big corporations and rich people, they have the money and money is all that matters in Washington. He said it is as if the men and women in the Congress and in the Senate put the gun in Simpson's hands."

"Are you saying he blamed the lawmakers?"

She looked at him and then at Benitez, but she didn't answer the question. "It's your turn, Agent Ready. Why are you here?"

He gave her a soft smile and directed her back to an easier topic, "Please, just give me a little more. What happened next?"

She nodded, again seeming to understand his tactic. "After about three weeks, I went back to work. They gave me an experienced aide, so that I could leave if I needed to; and I did, a lot at first. But being at work was good. It took my mind off what had happened. My friends thought it would be hard for me to be around kids, but it was good for me. But Greg never did that. I don't think he ever went back to work. His boss, Mr. Fryburg, he was so nice. He continued to pay Greg for a few weeks, but after it was clear Greg wasn't coming back, he had to stop."

"When did Mr. Hopper leave?"

"After about three months. We hardly spoke. I tried to engage him, but I think he felt guilty every time he saw me. One day I came home from work and he was gone. He left me a note. All it said was 'I'm sorry'." She started to cry again.

After she gathered herself Ready asked, "When did he call? Where was he? What did he say?"

"The first call was after a week or so. I had considered calling the police or hiring a private detective to find him, but I didn't. I thought he just needed to be on his own."

"Where did he call from?"

"He would never say exactly. I think the first time he just said he was out in the Midwest somewhere. He asked if I was doing all right and if I needed any money."

"Did he have money?"

"I don't know. I thought that was odd, too. I think he was working, just doing odd jobs to survive."

Ready noted that she had used the word *was*. "What else did you talk about?"

"There wasn't much. I tried to get him to come home at first, told him I loved him and that it wasn't his fault. But he would never really discuss it."

"When did you hear from him next?"

"About a month later. It was another short conversation. He asked if I was all right, if I needed anything. Again if I needed money."

Ready thought for a moment before asking his next question. He had a feeling that she knew why they were here. That she had nothing to hide and that she had the sense that soon they would know everything about them and that there was no point in holding back.

"Did you? Were you able to keep up on the bills without his income?"

She hesitated for a moment. "It has been a struggle." She paused again then went on. "Every once in a while, some deposits have shown up in my account. Some are from my mother, I think. But I'm pretty sure some are from Greg, too. As I said, I think he has been doing some work periodically."

"Were the amounts significant?"

The agents knew they would be going through her banking records as soon as they got the necessary subpoenas, and Sarah probably understood that as well.

"Most weren't. They helped, but most were $500 to $1,000. I think some of those were from my mom and maybe Greg's mom, too. But one was for almost $7,000."

Ready and Benitez exchanged glances. Benitez asked, "Could it have come from anyone else? Do you have any wealthy relatives?"

"No. None. I can't imagine who it could have been from, other than Greg. We asked every relative we could for help when we were trying to keep Jane in Middlebury. No one has that kind of money."

"When did you last hear from your husband? Did he ever say anything about making deposits?"

"It's been about six months, I think. And no. He never mentioned anything about making deposits. Most of the deposits started after that, after we last spoke. Maybe all of them, I'm not sure. The big deposit certainly did. It was only a couple of months ago."

"Did your husband say anything else?"

"Yes. The last time he called, he told me that I might start to hear things about him. I asked what he was talking about but he wouldn't say. He just said that I should know there's a reason for what he's doing. That it all had to mean something."

"Do you know what he meant by that?"

They paused for a moment and then Mrs. Hopper shrugged. He felt she knew, that they both knew, but she just couldn't say it.

She looked from Ready to Benitez then directed her question to Agent Ready. "Now will you tell me why you are here?"

Ready thought for a moment, considering whether he had any more questions. He looked to Benitez who simply nodded. Then he reached into his briefcase and pulled out a manila folder. From the folder he removed a single picture, the best one he had, from the parking garage under Mrs. Sinclair's apartment in Panama City. It was a picture that almost every person in the country had seen countless times.

Agent Ready handed the picture to Sarah. "Mrs. Hopper, is this your husband?"

Without hesitating she responded. "Yes."

Chapter 85

From Oakland, he headed up to Washington State to a small lumber town east of Tacoma. He found a job working at a mill and stayed at a $39 a night motel about fifteen miles away. He worked outside in the mill yard. It was dirty work so his face and arms were often covered in a thin layer of dust. He had been letting his hair and beard grow. He also wore tinted lenses that hid his eyes and always wore either a hard hat in the yard or a beat up old Pabst Blue Ribbon baseball cap. Even people who knew him would have trouble recognizing him.

Still, one night as he was sitting at a bar with two guys from work having a beer and trying to fit in, he was shocked to see a clear picture of his face flash across the TV screen. The picture was a close up of him, but from the tie he was wearing he recognized it as part of a digital family picture from Jane's graduation. They had zoomed in on his face and and cropped it.

As he stared at his image on the television screen, he was sure that the people around him would instantly recognize him and jump him or move away or at least find some excuse to leave their seats to make a phone call. But no one flinched. The bartender turned up the volume and the local news anchor explained that the man in the picture, Greg Hopper from Garden City, New York, was sought in connection with the congressional family killings. The anchor warned viewers not to approach the man if they saw him, but to call 911 or the FBI at the number shown at the bottom of the screen. After the news show moved to another story, the discussion at the bar turned to the killer and what people thought. Even in this gun owner-oriented part of the state, most said they hoped that they caught him before he killed again, but only after Congress was forced to pass the gun control legislation and not until after the election. It was the first time he, Hopper, had openly participated in a discussion since he sent his first letter to Williams at *The Erie Star*. Almost everyone in the discussion owned a gun, however all but two agreed with the proposed gun control legislation. It was reassuring for Hopper to hear. About 53% of Americans own guns, but between 80 and 90% favored the legislation. Even gun owners favored the legislation. Everyone at the bar agreed that term limits were a good idea.

Originally he only planned to stay for a beer or two, but after the picture came out, he decided to hang around, to hide in the open. He milked his beers though. The last thing he needed or wanted was a DUI.

Chapter 86

The debate in Congress was furious. Four days had passed since the gun control letter had been published and five since the date it was postmarked. The legislators wasted precious hours debating whether the two weeks started from the day the letter was mailed or the day it was published. After a five hour argument, they decided it was safer to go with the earlier date.

Every congressman, congresswoman and senator received thousands upon thousands of emails, letters and phone calls from their constituents. By a margin of about six to one, the petitions were in favor of the legislation. On top of that, it came out that many of the emails that opposed the gun control legislation were from bogus email addresses, likely sent in by people working for the NRA and other gun lobbies. A high percentage of the correspondence also openly favored term limits and made it clear that if the legislation didn't pass, the constituents intended to vote for the non-incumbent, in some cases even if it meant crossing party lines. Many added that they would vote against incumbents even if the legislation did pass.

Quietly and unbeknownst to the public, the legislators were also approached directly by lobbyists. Every single congressman was privately but legally offered at least $1 million for a negative vote on the gun legislation. Every senator was offered $2 million. They couched their language to make it legal, but representatives of the gun lobby were effectively offering more than $635 million for the "no" vote. The money would be "contributed" to each legislator's leadership PAC. Those PACs, which Congress created and made into law, allowed each congressman unfettered access to the funds. He or she could use the money to support cancer research or to pay for a family vacation. It was legal access to bribes. In some cases, especially with politicians who were up for re-election, the lobbyists used the argument that even if they did pass the gun control legislation, the momentum for term limits would probably mean that they were going to lose their seat anyway and possibly their benefits, so they should take the money while they could.

Chapter 87

After his first meeting with Sarah Hopper, Ready met with his bosses, eventually including the director of the FBI. The director was working with the attorney general and, through him, President Obama. They decided to release Hopper's picture and their version of his story almost immediately.

The Feds portrayed Hopper as a mad man. While the death of his daughter was tragic, his reaction was not sane. He was dangerous and unstable. No one should dare to approach him. He had killed eight innocent people with any number of weapons and was certain to be armed and extremely dangerous.

Behind the scenes, they considered him to be a rational, intelligent, extremely dangerous killer and an insurrectionist. *The New York Times* labeled him as the biggest threat to the republic since the civil war. And really, he was. He was undermining the entire system. Ready at least considered the idea he might not be acting alone.

The bureau got legal access to Sarah and Greg's financial records and tracked the payments into their account. Some of the smaller payments had in fact come from Sarah's mother. Others were deposited at ATMs at banks around the country. Those deposits were all made with cash. If Hopper was working, he was using aliases and either getting paid cash under the table or was cashing his paychecks elsewhere to get the currency for his deposits. The Feds visited each location where deposits were made and reviewed the video recordings at the ATMs. Some of the deposits were made before the release of the videos and stills from Mrs. Sinclair's parking garage in Panama City or from the motel in Missoula. Consequently, Hopper didn't go to any great lengths to hide his identity from the cameras. There was nothing illegal about making bank deposits and at that point, he wasn't on anyone's radar, so when he wasn't killing people or preparing to, he could appear publicly without disguising his identity. For the deposits made after the videos were released, he had both changed his appearance and done a good job of hiding his face from the cameras.

With new clearer pictures for facial recognition analysis and the records of his phone calls to Sarah, the Feds retraced what they knew of the killer's movements. New videos were found that placed him in motels and restaurants and at gas pumps in six additional states around the country. From the new videos, the Feds were able to piece together parts of his route and get a sense of how he operated. It seemed that generally Hopper was staying in cheap hotels or motels where he could pay cash or use debit "gift" cards to avoid leaving paper or electronic trails. It was possible that he might have had enough money to support his apparently frugal lifestyle. Additionally, there was some evidence that he had worked. A group of forest firefighters in Colorado were pretty sure he had spent several weeks working with them. The large deposit to Sarah's account had likely been funded from that work. His paychecks from the State of Colorado, made to a fictitious name and social security number, had been cashed at a check-cashing center in Medford, Oregon. Three days later, a man, who may or may not have been Hopper, deposited $6,800 into Sarah's checking account at an ATM in South Dakota.

During his killing spree, Hopper never showed any interest in collecting cash. With some of his victims, he apparently ignored wallets and purses that contained hundreds of dollars of cash. It was definitely possible that someone or some group was funding his operation. Maybe they were even planning it.

Chapter 88

As soon as the Feds released Greg's name as a suspect in the congressional family killings, Sarah's normal life ended. The street in front of her house became jammed with reporters, media trucks, gawkers and police officers all day, every day. Whenever she left the house, reporters bombarded her with questions and regular people screamed at her. She had to stop working and couldn't go anywhere without the police and the press following her. Her mother-in-law faced the same relentless hounding and scrutiny. Both received death threats.

However about a week after Hopper's identity became public, Mike Williams of *The Erie Star* wrote an article entitled, "For His Daughter's Sake". While Williams didn't condone Hopper's efforts, he did provide the public with an objective if not sympathetic outline of Greg's past few years. Once people became aware of what happened with the Reynolds Casino deal and how it led to Jane's transfer to Hofstra and the drive-by shooting and Jane's death, and the details of the lax gun laws that put the murder weapons that killed Jane Hopper into her killers' hands, there were also some offerings of support.

The FBI provided Sarah and her mother-in-law with around the clock protection.

Though she tried to deny it, Sarah knew all of this was coming for some time. Months earlier, when the first video of the Congressional Killer was released, Sarah immediately recognized the man as Greg. The video showed a man walking through a parking garage. It initially showed him from a distance then cut to a glimpse of his face, albeit from the side. Sarah hadn't really been paying attention to the news, but when she saw the video, before she knew what it was about or even saw the man's face, she recognized him as Greg. She could tell by his walk, by the way he carried himself. She wondered why he was on TV. Then she started to listen and realized that they suspected the man in the video, her husband, of being the Congressional Killer. It had been a total shock. She knew Greg was angry and had been worried that he might somehow try to retaliate, but that was in the immediate aftermath of Jane's death. Once the shooters were caught and the Donovan boy came to see them, she thought his anger had abated. She knew he blamed himself and would probably never be able to forgive himself, but it never occurred to her that he could kill innocent people. Even now, she couldn't believe he was capable of all of the horrible things he had done.

When she first saw the video she thought about his last phone call. He was warning her when he said that there was a reason for what he's doing. That it all had to mean something.

As the killings continued, her guilt and complicity became overwhelming at times. She wanted to call the authorities, to tell them the name of the man they were looking for, but she couldn't bring herself to do it. It seemed too disloyal and too final. Sarah was actually relieved the day the FBI agents came to her house.

She suspected that Greg's mother must have also known the video was of Greg, but they never discussed it. It was as if they both were too afraid to say it out loud, to tell anyone. After his name and the pictures were released she told her mother-in-law about Greg's last call.

Chapter 89

In the face of overwhelming voter demand, just one day before the Congressional Killer's deadline, a gun control bill was voted on in the Senate. That night, a slightly different version came before the House. Several of the legislators who were advocates of the bills were related to victims of the killer. One of strongest proponents and a co-sponsor of the Senate bill was Senator Bill Thompson of Connecticut, whose mother Evelyn had been murdered. The most vocal relative of a victim to publicly speak out against the legislation was Congressman David Sanford of Florida, whose ex-wife had been thrown from the fourteenth floor of her apartment building.

Both chambers' bills were watered-down products of compromise that bore little resemblance to the meaningful legislation that gun control advocates and the Congressional Killer were looking for.

On the day of the votes, there were rumors that the gun lobby had offered congressmen and congresswomen and senators almost a billion dollars to vote against the bills.

Neither bill passed. It wasn't even close.

Two days later a citizen in Cordova, Tennessee was found murdered in his home. The rifle with which he was shot was left beside his body. The license for the gun was taped to its stock. It had been purchased twelve hours before the body was found. Cordova was in the 9th Congressional District. His representative had been in Congress for thirty-two years and voted against the gun bill.

Chapter 90

There was a nationwide manhunt for Greg Hopper. His face was everywhere. Police forces across the country checked every hotel and motel for anyone even vaguely resembling him.

There was no sign of him.

Chapter 91

Four days after the gun bill failed and two days after the innocent citizen was murdered in Tennessee, Agent Ready called Sarah Hopper. In their pervious conversations, he had been courteous and respectful, but this time his tone was abrupt. He got straight to the point.

"Mrs. Hopper, I was just notified that two rather large payments were made on your behalf. Would you please explain what they are for? Who made them?"

"Payments? What sort of payments?"

"You don't know what I'm talking about?"

Her tone changed. She sounded irritated. "I have no idea, Agent Ready."

His gut told him she was telling the truth, but he didn't let it show. "Are you telling me you don't know that someone paid off your mortgages? Both of them?"

"Someone what? Who would do that?"

"This morning the two banks holding your mortgages each received wire transfers directed to your accounts. The transfers paid off the exact balances of your first and second mortgages. Are you telling me you don't know about it?"

She was silently dumbfounded on the other end.

"Mrs. Hopper?"

"I have no idea what you are talking about. Who would do that? Is it legal? Can someone just pay off someone else's mortgages?"

Ready spent ten more minutes questioning her, but either she didn't know anything about the payments or she was an amazing liar.

Chapter 92

Another three days passed and there was still no sign of Hopper. Ready and many of his superiors were convinced that someone was hiding him, consensually or not. Across the country, citizens were encouraged to be alert and to contact the police if they noticed friends or colleagues who were unexpectedly missing from work or school. Local police forces would then visit the missing people at home. When possible, they would ask to come inside to search the house or to see every family member, so that they could be sure they weren't being held hostage in their own homes.

Some of Ready's superiors also believed there might be some group, domestic or foreign, that was backing him. From the beginning, they conducted their investigation with that possibility in mind, but until the wire transfers, most believed the killer was operating independently.

The Bureau tracked the transfers. They came from the account of a newly formed LLC in Nevada, which was funded from a check from another newly formed entity in Kansas and so on and so on. Eventually they traced the funds through four different shell companies, to an account at a bank in the Cayman Islands and then to a Swiss account. The trail stopped there.

The convoluted nature of that paper trail made it appear that someone or some group, with deep pockets and a great deal of evasive sophistication, was, at the very least, in favor of Hopper's efforts. They were either working with him or condoning his efforts by anonymously financially supporting his wife.

The Feds did everything they could to tie what they knew of Hopper's movements to any other group or individual. They looked for people who had been in the same location as Hopper two or more times since the killings began in January. The more someone intersected with Hopper's activities, the more scrutiny he received. One man, Ted Larkin, had been in Panama City, Myrtle

Beach and near Summerset, Connecticut on the same days that they thought Hopper was there. Agents and police in his hometown of Hammersmith, Delaware spent days gathering information about him and hours and hours questioning him. It turned out that Larkin, who worked for a company that designed and made summer sportswear, simply had an unfortunate travel schedule.

The Feds also looked for recurring phone numbers, dialed from locations within a few hours of travel time of the murder sites that were made within hours or days of the relevant murder, but again had found nothing productive. Even if he was getting help and making phone calls to do it, he could make the calls to and from disposable phones and be effectively untraceable.

If there was a group backing or helping him, the FBI couldn't prove it.

They had to wait for him to come back out of hiding.

Chapter 93

Greg's appearance bore little resemblance to the pictures that were being widely circulated. He had long dark hair and a heavy graying beard and always wore glasses and often wore hats. But he tried to be careful not to look like a man hiding his appearance. He made a point of taking his hat off when he went inside and always looked people straight in the eye. He felt that if he was finally caught, at least it would all be over.

But in truth, it was fairly easy for him to hide in plain sight.

After he killed the innocent citizen in Tennessee, Greg drove to Austin, Texas and rented a cheap, furnished studio apartment. On the day he first saw and rented the place, he parked his car a few blocks away so that the complex manager and other tenants wouldn't see the make and model. He moved in on foot, with one duffle bag and a backpack, which wasn't unusual in the low-income, transient area. After he'd settled in, he walked back to his car and drove around until he found a used car dealer. He sold the Pathfinder for cash.

Two days later, he found a job washing dishes at an all night diner. He worked the night shift and some lunch hours. In his free time, he hung around in his apartment or at UT. The university was in session and he spent a lot of his time on the campus, reading or just walking around. He rode a cheap mountain bike everywhere he went. It kept him in shape and provided sort of an innocent cover.

One day as he was leaving to work a lunch hour shift, he saw one of his neighbors watching him. The neighbor was an older woman he had spoken with a couple of times. In their previous conversations, she asked him a lot of questions and he answered her vaguely, but he thought to her satisfaction. But when he saw her watching him again, he got a nervous feeling. He went back into his apartment and grabbed his backpack and some toiletries from the bathroom then went back out and hopped on his bike, as if he was going to work. Instead he rode to a fast food restaurant a few blocks away. He locked his bike on a rack there and walked back towards the apartment complex and sat in a window seat at a coffee shop across the street. An hour later, he saw a dark-colored sedan pull into the complex. The car parked in front of the woman's unit. When he saw two plainclothes officers or agents step from the car, he paid his bill and quickly left the restaurant.

In all of his months of killing and hiding, this was the closest he had come to the authorities. He found a cab and had the driver take him to the airport. He had to act fast. If the agents found the woman at all credible, there would be roadblocks around the city in no time.

He considered renting a car and driving, but needed to put as much distance as he could between himself and Austin. He had the cabbie drop him at the departure level. He wished he had the duffle bag he left in his apartment. Among other things, the bag contained material he used to disguise his appearance. While it would be handy to have, it might have been problematic at security. He didn't want to do anything to attract attention. He paid the taxi driver and walked inside, along the open hallway of the departure level, scouting the airline ticketing counters and kiosks. He made his way towards the end of the terminal, where the cheap commuter airlines had their counters. One airline, Lone Star Airways, looked especially pathetic. The kid behind the counter seemed bored and maybe high. He checked the airline's flight schedule, which consisted of white block letters and numbers on a black pegboard. The schedule showed flights to Houston every ninety minutes. The next flight was leaving in forty minutes, if the pegboard was up to date. He purchased a ticket using a different name than he had used while he lived in Austin. Then before going through security, he went into the men's room and into a stall. Using scissors and a hand mirror he kept in his backpack, he trimmed his beard and cut a few inches from his hair. He disposed of as much of the hair as he could in the toilet, flushing it several times. He also cut up and flushed the Idaho driver's license he used in Austin. He left the mirror on the floor behind the toilet and dropped the scissors in a garbage can in the outer terminal. He didn't have to worry about leaving fingerprints. The Feds and everyone else in the country knew his true identity.

Hopper went through security, handing the TSA agent a Rhode Island driver's license and his boarding pass. He intentionally removed his cap and scratched his head, looking the agent straight in the eye. The man smiled and handed the license and boarding pass back to Hopper. He put his cap back on and waited with the other travelers to get through security. As he approached the body scanners, he removed his cap, belt and shoes, but kept his glasses on. He couldn't believe that no one recognized him. The people around him were generally focused on watching their often valuable possessions on the conveyor belts and passing through the scanners themselves. The inspectors were more interested in what he was carrying on his person than in his face. He made it through security.

The flight was on time.

It took fifty minutes to reach Houston. He sat in a window seat in the back of the twin-engine, twelve-seat plane and spent most of the flight looking out the window. He felt sure he would be met by police as he deplaned, but wasn't. In Houston he took a cab into town and was dropped about five minutes from the bus station. He walked to the station and took a bus to Kansas City. In Kansas City he rented a car and disappeared.

Greg still hadn't decided what his endgame would be. He hoped to make it through the election, but wasn't sure what he would do if he did and his efforts failed. He did know that if it was possible, he wanted to make it back to New York for Election Day.

Chapter 94

For the first time since Senator Thompson's mother was murdered in Connecticut, Agent Ready felt as though he was actually on the killer's trail. Agents in Texas followed a lead and staked out an apartment in Austin where a woman claimed a man resembling Hopper lived. The woman believed the man she suspected worked in a restaurant, but she wasn't sure where. After watching the apartment for eleven hours without seeing any activity, the Feds got a warrant and entered. Inside they hit pay dirt.

The apartment, a seedy studio, had Hopper's prints all over it. He had apparently seen the agents because he disappeared, leaving a packed duffle bag full of clothes and personal belongings behind. There was nothing especially telling or incriminating among the clothes, though they did find some things he must have used to disguise his identity, including several fake beards and a false belly.

With an updated composite drawing of his appearance from the female neighbor's description, they were able to find the restaurant, a diner, where he worked and eventually trace him to a flight with a small commuter airline from Austin to Houston. From there, his trail dried up again.

Chapter 95

So long as he was in the car on highways, Greg felt almost invisible. It was stopping to eat or sleep or even to go to the bathroom that was problematic.

When he first started to hide, he tended to stay in low-income, rough areas. But with experience and especially after Austin, he felt safer in slightly nicer areas. People in really poor areas were more familiar with crime and criminals and seemed more aware of unusual people or activities. So after Austin, Greg tried to stop in more affluent looking towns or in office parks, when he had to stop at all. He still stayed in cheap motels along highways in those areas, checking in late at night and leaving in the late morning, after most of the one night business travelers who typically populated those types of motels were long gone. He ate at drive-thru fast food restaurants and gassed up at automated pumps, keeping his head down and cap on, to avoid security cameras. Generally, when he did have to interact with people, so long as he was friendly and quick he felt he could go unnoticed. But he knew that would only last until one person became suspicious, so he kept his interactions to a bare minimum. He worked his way east from Kansas City, towards home.

Chapter 96

Two days after Hopper's trail dried up in Houston, a woman called the FBI hotline. The woman, Theresa Helman, of Williston, North Dakota, claimed she sat next to Hopper on a bus from Little Rock, where she had been visiting her sister, to Kansas City. She said that Hopper got off in Kansas City.

Helman explained that she couldn't read in a car or bus so she wasn't paying attention to the news and hadn't seen the recent pictures and composite drawings of Hopper. When she finally got home, she went right to bed and slept for ten straight hours. So it wasn't until she watched the news the next morning, a day and a half after Hopper got off the bus in Kansas City, that she realized who he was. The instant she saw the picture, she was positive she had been sitting next to the Congressional Killer and immediately called the FBI.

Within hours, agents descended on Kansas City and eventually discovered that Hopper had in fact been there and that he rented a black Toyota Camry, which was one of the most commonly driven cars in the country. They had no idea where he went from there.

Chapter 97

By the time the agents discovered that Greg was driving a Camry, he had a plan to dispose of it. Before he even left Kansas City, he went to the long-term lot at the airport and swapped his Kansas plates with those of a dark gray Ford Focus parked there.

He drove east along I-70, putting as much distance as he could between himself and the Feds. He stopped in Columbus, Ohio to change cars again. He parked the Camry in an indoor parking garage in the city and caught a bus to the airport. He went to the rental car area at the airport and rented a dark gray Chrysler 200 using his last fake driver's license. This one had him as a resident of Nevada.

From Columbus, Greg continued east towards his next destination, New Hampshire, to a friend's parents' cottage. He visited the cottage in about 1995. It was secluded and at the time, his friend's family kept an SUV there. He was pretty sure they still did.

The cottage was on Squam Lake in central New Hampshire, northwest of Lake Winnipesaukee. Greg remembered that the cottage had an extremely long driveway and the house itself could only be seen from the lake. He figured that in late October there wouldn't be much boat traffic, especially in the shallow secluded cove where the cottage sat. The house itself wasn't winterized, but there had always been a bunch of sleeping bags in the bunkrooms and down comforters in the bedrooms.

If the owners, the Bennetts, weren't there, it would be a great place for him to stay and hide. If they were, he would just turn around and leave, hopefully unnoticed. He stocked up on supplies in Springfield, Massachusetts on the way up and felt he had enough food and water to get him through Election Day, wherever he was.

Once he reached Squam, he parked his car on the Bennetts' long driveway about a third of a mile and a few bends from the house and walked the rest of the way, so that he wouldn't be seen if anyone was home. Before he was within fifty yards of the house, he was pretty sure it was empty and had been for sometime. As he got closer, he saw there were leaves and small branches on the front stoop and in front of the side door. They were the only practical entrances from the dirt driveway. If anyone had been there, they would have used one of those doors and certainly would have at least moved the branches to the side. Even so, he walked around the house, looking for signs of life and for a way in.

The building was a brown shingle, early seventies type A-frame, with a great room with thirty-foot ceilings and bunks rooms upstairs to either side of the central peak. The front and back of the house had huge pane windows that provided great views from inside, and easy viewing from outside. After he was sure no one was inside, he went into the unlocked screened porch off the kitchen. He tried the window over the kitchen sink that looked out into the porch. Its lock was weak and he easily broke it. He moved a rocker to the front of the window and climbed in.

The house was pretty much the way he remembered it. It was a big, very casual cottage. He didn't think anyone had been inside in some time. When he opened the fridge, it was on and there was some food inside; things like ketchup and olives, non-perishables, would last, but there were no perishables like milk or cheese or cold cuts or fruits or vegetables. Someone had cleaned the fridge for the winter. He felt he was safe, for a while at least.

Next Greg checked the garage. There was an old Chevy Tahoe parked inside. He found the keys in a drawer in a workbench. The truck started right up when he tried it. It was perfect. He could drive it anonymously. He cut the engine and opened the door. As he stepped from the SUV, he turned to see the barrel of a rifle pointing at his face.

"Stop right there."

Greg looked past the barrel to the face of an old man. He stood still between the open driver's side door and the truck itself.

"What are you doing here?"

"I'm a friend of the Bennetts. Young Bill told me I could stay here."

"I just watched you crawl through the kitchen window."

"Bill forgot to give me the key. I talked to him and he told me the kitchen window would be unlocked, that I could get in through there."

"Bullshit. I saw you break the lock. And they hide a key and anyone who talked to them would know where it is. Besides, I saw you checking every door and window and looking inside before you broke in."

As the man was speaking, Hopper saw recognition in his eyes and then fear. He raised his hands and stepped towards him.

"Don't take another step. I know who you are."

"Who do you think I am?"

The old man shuffled back a few feet. "You're Greg Hopper. You're the guy who has been killing all of those innocent people."

"I'm not." He took another step forward.

"One more step and I'll shoot. Stop right there..."

Before he could finish his sentence, Greg lunged to his right and forward. To his complete surprise, the man fired at him, catching him in his left shoulder. The impact of the bullet pushed his left side back but he continued forward, leading with his right shoulder. The old man tried to aim at him again but Greg knocked the barrel to the side and drove forward, tackling him. He was on him in an instant, on his chest and torso. The old guy tried to fight, to buck him off, but quickly realized it was pointless. Greg pinned him down, with a knee on each of his boney shoulders.

"You shot me."

Still straddling him, he felt his left shoulder with his right hand. He winced in pain when he touched it. The old man saw him wince and tried to push him off again. Greg didn't budge.

"Stop it. Don't move. I don't want to hurt you."

"The hell you don't. You've killed, what, eight or nine people."

"I don't want to add you to the list." He looked down at him and said, "I'm done killing." Greg reached over and picked up the rifle. Slowly he stood, first leaving a knee on the man's chest and then a lightly placed foot. He stepped back from him, holding the rifle and looking at his shoulder. The man started to get up.

"Don't move." He didn't even look up as he spoke. He just examined his shoulder.

"What are you going to do to me?"

Hopper looked down at him again. "I'm not going to hurt you. I just need to give myself some time." He touched his finger to the gash in his shoulder and winced again, then said, "Get up. Let's go inside."

He followed the man into the house, through the side door. To the right of the door was a utility room with a washer and dryer, a wall of tools and several piles of summer sporting goods. Greg stood behind the man, looking out the window towards the driveway to see if any neighbors were coming in reaction to the gunshot.

"What's your name?"

"It's Miller." The man's voice was full of disdain.

"Okay, Mr. Miller, here's what we're going to do. I want you to go in there and sit on the floor with your back to the washer." He pointed to the utility room with the barrel of the rifle.

Miller went in and sat. Greg saw him look at the tools on the pegboard and the tool bench. "Just stay there. Don't move."

Greg rummaged through the tool bench until he came up with a brand new coil of white rope, over 150 feet. He took the rope and a box cutter and led Miller out into the great room.

"I have to tie you up so that I can tend to this." He pointed at his shoulder, which was bleeding heavily.

Several railroad tie style 8″ by 8″ pillars supported the upstairs balcony that ran along the front of the great room, connecting the bedrooms on the left side of the house to the stairway and bedrooms on the right. Greg motioned to the center pillar. "Sit on the floor with your back to that, legs out flat."

Hopper watched as the old man struggled to sit down again. He took two cushions from the couch in the room and tossed them to Miller. "Here. Sit on one and put the other between your back and the pillar. Lean back against it."

The old man looked up, a little surprised. Once Miller was seated

Hopper rested the rifle against the couch behind him and started to uncoil the rope. He tied one end into a loop with a slipknot and put the loop over Miller's feet and around his ankles, then pulled it tight.

"Hold your hands together behind your back, behind the pillar."

Once the old man's hands were in position, he pulled the slipknot around his ankles tighter and tied it off. Then he walked around Miller and the pillar about ten times, tying his upright torso to the pillar. He cut the end of the rope and tied it off. Finally he tied Miller's wrists together, wrapping them six or seven times.

"That ought to hold you for a while."

Hopper checked the binds and then picked up the rifle and headed towards the master bedroom, which was on the first floor across the great room from the kitchen. He rummaged through the cupboards in the master bath until he found an old first aid kit. He took the kit and a sewing kit and went back out to the great room, holding the rifle with his wounded left arm.

He spent about thirty minutes cleaning the wound and trying to stitch it, using a needle from the sewing kit and fishing line he found in the utility room. The bullet passed through the fleshy part of his shoulder and hadn't seemed to hit any bone. While it hurt like crazy, Greg didn't think it was too serious. He tried to stitch it up, but couldn't bring himself to push the needle through his raw, open flesh more than a few times on each side of the gash.

Leaving the rifle against the couch, well out of Miller's reach, he went back into the bedroom and came back with strips of bed sheet. He covered the wound with antiseptic and gauze from the first aid kit and then tied the strips of sheets around his arm, to hold the gauze in place.

Once he was finished, he turned his attention back to Miller. "Where did you come from?"

Miller nodded to a house on the point at the entrance to the cove. The house was on the opposite side of the cove from the Bennetts' driveway. If he walked, chances are he hadn't seen Greg's car, which was still parked well up the driveway, hidden from view.

"How did you get here? Why did you even come?"

"I saw you walking around the Bennetts' house, looking in the windows. I figured you were up to no good, so I walked over to catch you."

Greg hoped he was telling the truth and that he hadn't called the cops before he came to investigate. Now he would have to stick with the Chrysler. There was a good chance the old guy hadn't seen it.

"I'm going to have to leave you tied up for a while. Do you think you'll be okay? Are you comfortable?"

"No, I'm not comfortable."

Hopper nodded. "I guess not." He sat on the couch for a while, to think things through. Then he walked back to Miller and searched his pockets. He found a wallet and a cell phone. He checked the call history on the phone. There were no calls in the past three hours. He hadn't called the police, at least not from his cell.

"I'm going to have to leave you here like this, for four or five hours. Do you think you can handle that?"

Miller shrugged his shoulders.

"I just need some time to get away from here."

He left Miller and rummaged around the cottage for a while.

After about fifteen minutes, he came back into the great room with a glass of water. He held the glass in front of Miller's face, a couple inches from the old man's lips. "You might want to drink this. As I said, I need some time to get away, so you are going to be stuck here for a while. Do you want some water? Are you thirsty?"

Miller nodded and Greg brought the cup to Miller's lips and slowly tilted it, letting Miller drink as much as he wanted, at his own pace.

"In four or five hours, I will make a call and get you some help." He fumbled though Miller's wallet. "Are you married? Do you want me to call your wife or the police?"

Miller shrugged.

"It's up to you. It might be faster if I call your wife, but who knows. Is she over at your house?"

"My wife is dead. Why don't you just call the police?" His voice was filled with disgust as he spoke. "As if you are going to call anyone."

"Okay. Is it the Meredith PD or is there a closer police station? In Center Harbor or Holderness?"

"Holderness."

"Okay, I'll call them as soon as I feel I'm safely away."

After Miller finished drinking, Greg stood and walked over to the rifle. He removed the bullets, including the one that was in the chamber. Initially he put them in his pocket, but then decided it didn't matter and placed them on a table and leaned the rifle against the couch. He checked the binds and knots. Satisfied that it would be very difficult and time consuming for Miller to free himself, he stood. He grabbed a blanket from the couch and draped it over the old man. He tossed Miller's wallet on the floor beside him, but kept his phone. Finally Greg grabbed a few things from an upstairs bedroom and went outside. Three or four minutes later, Miller heard the sound of car doors opening and closing then heard a car start. It sounded like the car was a little way up the Bennetts' driveway. A minute later, he heard it drive away.

Two and a half hours later, as he was passing from New Hampshire into Massachusetts on I-93, Hopper called the Holderness Police Department from Miller's phone. He told the officer who answered that there was a man, James Miller, who needed help inside the Bennett house on Old Harvard Road on Squam Lake. He said it was an emergency. Then he hung up, turned off the phone and took out its battery.

Greg had gone to New Hampshire with two objectives: to hide for a few days and to steal the Bennetts' SUV. The trip was a disaster. He wasn't sure if the Feds had been able to trace him to Kansas City or knew that he had rented a Camry, but he had to assume they did. He hoped they didn't know that he had changed the plates or that he was now driving a Chrysler.

He took 495 East and then caught I-95 North towards Maine.

Chapter 98

An hour later, Ready received word that Hopper had a run in with an elderly man in central New Hampshire. The man, James Miller, apparently caught Hopper breaking into a deserted summer cottage and cornered him in a garage. Miller, who was in his late seventies, tried to hold him at gunpoint, but Hopper charged him. The old man fired a shot and hit him. Unfortunately, he only grazed his shoulder. Hopper overpowered Miller and tied him up in the house. Then, remarkably, after he felt he was safely away, Hopper called a police station in a town near the cottage and told them to go rescue the old guy.

Ready's first instinct was to trace the call to the police department. Hopper used the old man's cell to make the call, so while the identity of the caller wouldn't help, isolating the cell tower the phone had accessed to make the call would. Unfortunately that always took time. Ninety minutes later he learned that the call had gone through a cell tower in Lowell, Massachusetts. He was heading south.

Chapter 99

The news that Hopper had finally been sighted and that he had actually been shot was all over the internet and on the twenty-four hour news stations. It was the lead story on all of the networks evening news programs.

Sarah was watching NBC news with her mother. A female reporter from NBC's Concord, New Hampshire affiliate was on site at a cottage in New Hampshire where an older man, James Miller, had seen Hopper snooping around a neighbor's property, a summer home, and had gone to investigate. The reporter was actually interviewing the old guy.

Miller explained that he surprised Hopper in the Bennetts' garage and held him at gunpoint, but that Hopper charged him. Sarah's heart skipped a beat when he said he got a shot off and hit him. Miller said that as Hopper lunged forward he pushed the gun's barrel to the side, so that the shot only grazed his shoulder. Momentum carried Hopper forward. He tackled the old man and took the gun.

When the reporter asked what happened next, the old guy smiled and said, "It was the darnedest thing. This killer, he took me inside and tied me up, but he gave me a pillow to sit on and to put another one between my back and the pillar I was tied to. Then he got me a glass of water and a blanket."

She urged him to continue.

"He asked me some questions and left. I think he was planning to steal the Bennetts' truck. He was checking to see if it worked when I caught him in their garage. But he didn't take it. And he left me my rifle, too. Only thing he took was my cell phone. He said he was going to call the cops to tell them where I was. I didn't believe him of course. He walked out of the house and a few minutes later I heard a car start and drive away. I guess he had one up the driveway a bit, hidden from the house."

"He had me tied up so tight I thought I might be there forever.

But sure enough, about three or four hours later, I heard a car pull into the driveway."

The reporter asked who it was.

"I was afraid it might be him, coming back to finish me off. But it was one of the local cops, Bill Patterson. He called my name from outside and I shouted back 'Here I am'. Hopper actually called the cops and told them to come get me."

The old guy scratched his head and looked at the young reporter. "Why in the world would a killer do that?"

She asked, "Did he say anything else?"

"Yeah. He said he was done killing."

Chapter 100

Greg drove north along I-95 through coastal New Hampshire towards Maine then used Route 1 to avoid the toll plazas along the interstate in southern Maine. He intended to get back onto 95, but ended up taking the scenic route along Route 1 all the way up the coast towards Bar Harbor. He felt safe and anonymous driving, especially on rural roads at night.

He listened to news radio along the way and heard an interview with the old man who'd shot him, Mr. Miller. Hopper was glad to hear him say he "guessed" that he had a car up the driveway. Unless the FBI told him to say it, to give Hopper a false sense of security, it meant that there was still a good chance they didn't know what kind of car he was driving.

His plan in Maine was similar to what it had been in New Hampshire. Years earlier, he and Sarah visited a friend's summerhouse in Sorrento, which was a beautiful, craggy coastal town on Sullivan Harbor near Bar Harbor. Greg knew of two cottages there. One was newer and likely to have an alarm system, but the other was a true, old style summer cottage. It was completely isolated and he felt sure that if he could make it up there and get in, it would be a safe place to wait.

At about 8 pm, he turned off Route 1 near Sorrento and found his way to West Shore Road. Even in the summer there wasn't much traffic on the rural road, but at this time of year it was really dead.

Greg found the driveway he was looking for and turned in. If he remembered correctly, the house was set about half a mile back from the road. As he had in New Hampshire, he figured he would drive about a quarter of a mile in and then walk the rest of the way, to be sure there wasn't anyone in the house. It was a clear moonlit night so he turned off his headlights. After letting his eyes adjust for a minute, it was easy for him to slowly find his way along the meandering dirt road. The driveway pitched sharply lower as he approached the cottage, which was by the water.

Greg found the cottage dark and empty. He hoped to come and go without leaving a trace, but had to break a window to get in.

Chapter 101

After the flurry of activity around Austin and Kansas City and at the cottage in New Hampshire, the public and Congress again expected the situation to finally be resolved, and quickly. Agent Ready hoped so too, but three days passed and there was no new news on Hopper.

The Feds, state and local police crews, hospitals and even doctors were on full alert. There was no sign of him anywhere.

Since they discovered the killer's identity, Ready and his team were monitoring Sarah's activities and all of her communication. As far as they could tell, she was neither in touch with her husband nor helping to harbor him. But they also knew that she wasn't exactly forthcoming with information. After Greg's attempt to hide at the cottage in New Hampshire, the Feds used Sarah's online contacts and phone records to reach out to her friends, asking about any secluded spots they might have visited with Greg or Sarah.

Among other places, they learned of a cottage the Hoppers visited years earlier in northeastern Maine, near Bar Harbor.

Chapter 102

Sarah was pretty sure she knew where Greg was.

In 2005, when Jane was about ten, she and Greg spent a long weekend in northern Maine with their friends the Parkers. The Parkers' house was totally secluded. It was possible Greg was there, but Sarah doubted it. Ben Parker, their friend, loved gadgets and all things electronic. It drove his wife Jackie crazy. Sarah felt sure that Ben would have the house wired with a great alarm system. There is no way Greg would risk tripping that. But when they were up visiting the Parkers, Jackie and Ben took them to a cocktail party at a neighbor's house. While Sarah and Greg loved the Parkers' house, it was beyond what they ever imagined they could afford to spend on a cottage, even when they daydreamed. But they always loved the little cottage where Parkers took them for the cocktail party. In their view, it was the perfect summerhouse.

The more Sarah thought about it, the more she was sure that Greg was there. She wanted to drive up to see him, to talk to him and convince him to stop. But she couldn't risk even calling him. She was sure the Feds were watching her and that her phones and those of anyone she could trust were being tapped. There was just no way.

Chapter 103

Maine State Troopers Matt Feighery and Matt Hannon, known at the barracks as Young and Old Matt, were sent to check out the summerhouse of Ben and Jackie Parker on West Shore Road in Sorrento.

As they pulled into the Parkers' dirt driveway, they shared the apprehensive rush that policemen frequently feel. More often than not, routine searches turned out to be nothing. But officers know there is always the potential for something more. And in this case, there was a remote possibility that Matt and Matt might find the most wanted man in America. While the officers tried not to show it, each man could feel a surge of adrenaline as they approached the house.

The Parkers' house was built on a ridge, about two hundred feet above Sullivan Bay. The driveway ran along a higher plateau, about seventy feet above the house, so that as the officers came over the crest of the hill, above the house, they were able to get a good look at the property. The house looked empty. It was about 5:15 pm and the sun was still out, but low in the sky, directly behind the house. There were no lights on inside and no signs of any activity.

Feighery stopped the car at the top of the hill as Hannon called in their position. The two officers cautiously made their way down the rest of the driveway on foot, towards the house. Against normal procedure, each man had his gun drawn with the safety off. They went to the front door and looked in the windows. The lights were off, but the sun was shining through the house from the horizon across the bay, providing the officers with a clear look through the open first floor. The rooms looked empty and there was no sign of recent use. Sheets covering the furniture were still in place and fairly taut across the arms. From what they could see, it didn't look as if anyone had been sitting on the couches or chairs. Likewise the counters appeared clear.

Young Matt pointed his gun towards the doorbell and looked to

Old Matt. The senior officer shook his head and brought a finger to his lips. He pointed at Feighery and motioned to the right side of the house. Then he pointed at himself and to his left. The younger officer nodded and the two men slowly proceeded along their respective sides. They looked in all of the windows and checked for any sign of activity. Neither saw anything.

They met at the back of the house, on a huge slate patio that overlooked the bay. The officers agreed that it seemed unlikely that anyone was living inside. Still, because they couldn't go inside and properly check all of the rooms, they weren't sure and both remained on edge.

Young Matt pointed with his gun again, this time towards a second, smaller house down by the water. Old Matt nodded and they headed down a steep stone stairway to a meandering slate path that led to the boathouse and the water.

Chapter 104

Hopper was able to regroup at the cottage by the water. During the day, he relaxed in a sunny spot on the inland side of the house or simply slept on a bed inside. He had been able to put a few more stitches into the gash in his shoulder and while it wasn't pretty, it was clean and the graze wound was closed.

At night, he slept or sat in the living room, looking out over the bay. He left the lights off.

He kept up with the news by listening to the radio and, during daylight hours, occasionally watching TV. After several days of no sightings, the manhunt for him had grown too dull for ongoing coverage, but with the election looming, his agenda had not. Candidates' views and pledges on term limits and gun control were projected to be major variables in individual race outcomes and those favoring each were often viewed as frontrunners.

On his third day at the cabin, Greg decided to go for a walk. So long as he stayed away from the road and the water, he felt safe. He made his way up the steep hill from the lake through the woods in the general direction of the Parkers' house. When he had visited about ten years earlier, the house was new. He was curious to see how it had changed over the years.

After about five minutes of walking uphill towards the northeast, the house came into view. It appeared empty. From the woods, he cautiously made his way closer. There was a strong breeze coming up from the water, so there was a lot of rustling of trees and branches and dry leaves. He didn't think anyone was around and was confident that even if someone was, the sounds from the wind would more than cover any noise he made.

He got to the edge of the woods by the front of the house and stood there for a few minutes. There was no sign of human activity. He felt safe and walked out onto the driveway and took a good look at the house.

It was beautiful. His friend Ben had designed it himself and Greg was really impressed. For a moment, he forgot his circumstances and looked forward to telling Ben how incredible it all was. He walked around the left side of the house towards the back patio.

Chapter 105

The officers checked out the boathouse and again found nothing. From the dock, they could see another small cottage by the water, further down the bay. It appeared empty as well.

They relaxed and made their way back up the path.

Chapter 106

As Greg walked back towards the patio, along the side of the house he relaxed and peeked in the windows. The inside was as beautiful as the outside. Greg imagined how nice it would be to spend summers here.

From the back patio, he could see the sun starting to set across the bay. The view was incredible. There were several Adirondack chairs by the back railing. He decided to sit in one and watch the sunset.

As he approached the railing, he was astonished to hear the sound of two men talking. They were below him, but very close. He turned to hurry back up the slope towards the front of the house. When he looked up, he stopped dead in his tracks. A Maine State Patrol car parked just up the driveway, facing him. The car had been hidden by trees when he had first approached the house from the side, but was clearly visible now. For a second, Greg was sure that he was caught. But nothing happened. He didn't see any officers inside the cruiser.

From behind, he heard the sounds of the men's feet on the steps leading up to the patio. He panicked and sprinted towards the front of the house, then to his left, back to the cover of the woods. Once he was about forty feet in, he ducked behind a thick pine and waited. He heard and then saw two state troopers walk up to the car. His heart raced.

After about two minutes, they drove away.

The authorities must have spoken with the Parkers. He hoped they hadn't mentioned that Hopper had also visited the small cottage down by the bay. If the officers did check the cottage, he was finished. His Chrysler with Ohio plates was parked in front of the cottage, next to the owner's old Taurus wagon. If they ran the plates, they would discover it was a recent rental and within an hour, the area would be crawling with cops.

He considered his options. Without a car he didn't stand a chance. Even with one, it would only be a matter of time before he was caught.

There were only three roads out of Sorrento and the authorities would have them blocked before he could get far. Greg decided to run back towards the small cottage and wait. He ran southwest through the woods until he reached the cottage's driveway. Then, staying to one side, he made his way down the driveway to the bay. When he was about one hundred feet from the cottage, he found a spot that gave him a good view of both the cottage and the driveway and waited, hidden in the woods about fifteen feet in from the road.

An hour later, he was confident that the officers weren't going to check "his" cottage. He went back inside.

Chapter 107

With the information gathered from Sarah's contacts, the Feds and local authorities checked all of the places they knew of that the Hoppers had visited over the years. Police checked homes, cabins and hotels from South Carolina to Maine and even one cottage in Ontario. Ready was beyond frustration. They were so close. He couldn't believe that Hopper had slipped through their net, again. By now, he could be anywhere.

Chapter 108

Three nights later, the night before the election, Greg left the cottage in Maine just after sunset. He was driving the 1996 green Ford Taurus wagon he'd found parked in the driveway.

Chapter 109

Two weeks after the gun legislation failed, on November 3rd 2014, Senator Bill Thompson of Connecticut asked for airtime on every major network and cable news station. He issued a statement saying that he and a number of his colleagues in the House and Senate would like a chance to address the American people on the night before Election Day.

He stood at a podium flanked by almost a dozen congressional colleagues including three who had lost relatives. Neither Senator Adam Keating of New York nor Representative David Sanford of Florida was present. In the preamble to the Senator's remarks, members of the media were at a loss as to Thompson's agenda. They did speculate that he would discuss the failed gun control legislation, but couldn't come up with a good reason for doing it so publicly or in such an unusual venue. The news conference was being held in his mother's home in Summerset Connecticut, in what must have been his father's office. She had been murdered about fifty feet away, in her family room.

There was a real air of anticipation, as if something big was about to unfold, but no one could get a handle on what it was.

Thompson looked a little stiff as he stood before the podium.

"My fellow Americans, tonight we stand on the eve of one of the most extraordinary midterm elections in our nation's history. For the past nine months, a man has been terrorizing our country. None of us, and no right-thinking man or woman in this country condones his actions, but many of us, myself included, believe that Congress has become ineffective and that it is time for some drastic changes.

"Two weeks ago, in spite of overwhelming support from you, our citizens, for the second time since twenty-six people, including twenty school children, were murdered in Newtown, Connecticut, the House and Senate voted overwhelmingly against common sense gun legislation. There have been reports in the media that the gun lobby offered senators and congressmen incredible sums of money to vote against the legislation.

"Those rumors are true. I was offered over $4 million to vote against the bill. Senator Drinkwater was offered over $2 million and Congressman Boeckh was offered over $1 million. Every congressman and woman and every senator standing here was offered at least those amounts."

He turned and acknowledged each man when he mentioned his name and then the entire group.

"It is our understanding that at least $2 million was offered to every senator and at least $1 million was offered to every congressman in Washington. Think of that.

"Whether everyone who voted against the bill took the money I can't say, but the fact is, we were all offered money for our votes. And, perhaps more remarkably, we would not be breaking any laws by accepting that money. Because of self-serving laws enacted and supported by a vast majority of Congress, including some of us standing here, we are allowed to accept money from lobbyists to do with as we please, legally.

"The offers of money, of bribes to vote against the gun bill came from the gun lobby, specifically backed by the National Rifle Association and by virtually every gun and ammunition manufacturer in this country and in many parts of the world.

"Everyone here voted for the bill and none of us accepted the money, the bribes. But we all, each of us here, have accepted so-called legal contributions to our Leadership PACs in the past. And we all admit that those contributions did influence our votes.

"The fact that accepting these bribes is somehow viewed as legal shows how far things have gone astray. Congressional approval ratings have hovered in the low to mid teens for years. Since the failure of the gun legislation, they are down to mid-single digits. Ninety-five percent of you think we are totally ineffective.

"I agree with you. Everyone standing here does. For years, we have been fighting wars that no one wants and spending money that we don't have. Many of us standing here disagree on how to solve our problems or even on what the problems are, but we do agree that our system is broken.

"Unless we want to continue to let our country deteriorate, we have to make some major changes.

"To all of us, term limits seem like a great and necessary first step. And they are a major step. We are all long-serving congressmen and congresswomen and senators. Frankly, we have been here for too long. Two of the senators standing here are not up for election tomorrow, so it is possible that even if there is a strong vote against incumbents in tomorrow's elections, they could ride it out. But they won't. None of us will seek re-election. Not me or Senator Drinkwater or the congressmen and congresswomen standing here. Nine of us are up for re-election tomorrow, but we are removing our names from the ballots. If it is too late and we are re-elected, we will not be sworn in and will not serve our terms. It is time for new people to try to fix our problems. We have had our chance and frankly and obviously, we have failed.

"I will not ever seek elected office again. Not the seat I have occupied in the Senate, not a seat in the House and not the Presidency. I have had my chance and I failed. The men and women standing behind me will make similar pledges, but I will leave that to them.

"We encourage everyone who is voting tomorrow to vote against incumbents, no matter what party they represent.

"Many of you believe that doing that, voting against incumbents, would be condoning the actions of a murderer. Many feel that if they vote specifically against their incumbents, they will be saying that these killings have been merited, that they were somehow serving the greater good.

"We will never condone taking a single life and we don't tonight. But we *do* recognize that things need to change. When Congress can't pass bills that 90% or more of the citizens of this country want, especially something as obviously good and right as the gun control legislation that failed two weeks ago, something is wrong with our system. When we can spend a decade in a series of wars that our citizens don't want and that we cannot afford and that we cannot win, something is wrong with our system. When year after year we run deficits in the trillions of dollars and saddle our children and grandchildren and perhaps our great-grandchildren with insurmountable mountains of debt, something is wrong with our system. When our elected officials are so beholden to special interests and to lobbyists and unions and to our own political parties that we can no longer vote with our conscience, something is wrong. And when legislators can legally accept bribes to vote a certain way, something is clearly wrong.

"There is no single quick fix that will solve all of our problems. But as it stands, the United States Congress is an ineffective body. One can argue that it has been for decades. We need to make significant changes. Those of us standing here believe that term limits are a necessary and potentially incredibly positive change. Elections in this country have become so expensive and so time consuming that most legislators spend more time working on getting re-elected than they do on legislative issues. Special interests groups are the only beneficiaries of the constant focus on re-election. They contribute to election campaigns, but do so with strings. On top of that, in order to gain access to worthwhile committees and to be endorsed for re-election, freshman and junior congressmen and congresswomen and senators must bow to the wishes of their party leadership rather than voting their conscience.

"Term limits directly address those issues. Congressmen and congresswomen and senators should serve one six-year term. Really effective legislators could serve in both the House and the Senate and serve a total of twelve years. Freed from obligations to campaign contributors and lobbyists, past and future, and freed from demands to vote along party lines to gain access to committees controlled by long-serving senior legislators, elected officials could truly vote for what they believe is right.

"There is a real need for debate on how to restructure the United

States Congress to make it effective, but it seems very clear that the current Congress is not composed of men and women who are willing to debate such issues, let alone make the changes necessary to put our country back on the right track. This Congress cannot even act on behalf of their constituents on something as universally supported as the recent gun control bills.

"But tomorrow, you, the American people, can make that change. Tomorrow when you vote, please vote against any incumbent, no matter what party he or she is in. It is time to look beyond partisan politics. It is time for change.

"Collectively, you have the power to make the changes we desperately need. Please don't vote for any incumbents.

"We can do better than this. Vote for someone new. Almost one hundred percent of the candidates seeking first terms tomorrow have signed pledges to not serve more than six years in the House or Senate. They want change. They believe in term limits. When you go to the voting booth tomorrow, think of the failed votes in the House and in the Senate two weeks ago. Think of the hundreds of millions of dollars in payoffs.

"Please don't vote for any incumbent.

"We can do better than this. Tomorrow, when you vote, think of the children of Sandy Hook Elementary, the people of Aurora, of Columbine, the students at Virginia Tech and of so many other innocent victims. Think of the hundreds of millions of dollars that went into the pockets of politicians two weeks ago. Think of the wars we have fought, of the deficits we are running and of the debt burden we are placing on our children.

"We can do better than this, so much better. Please don't vote for any incumbent."

Chapter 110

The next day, Election Day, thirty-three seats in the Senate and all four hundred and thirty-five seats in the House of Representatives were contested.

Chapter 111

Agent Ready and the Feds had no idea where Hopper was. While there had been many false leads, there hadn't been a single legitimate sighting or bit of new evidence since Hopper called the police department near Squam Lake.

That incident had the Feds and every reporter in the country confused. Since the failure of the gun control legislation, pretty much every person in the United States who wasn't a congressman or senator was fair game. So why hadn't he killed Miller?

Ready believed it was because Miller wasn't part of the plan. Hopper had methodically plotted out each killing and each had served a purpose, his purpose. Miller's death wouldn't have. The old man just happened upon Hopper as he was trying to steal a car. He wasn't sure if it mattered or if the outcome would have been different if the one person who found him hadn't been an old man whom he could easily overpower. But Ready had a sense that Hopper had been telling the truth when he told Miller he was done killing.

Chapter 112

It took Greg eleven hours to drive from northeastern Maine to New York City. He took his time and occasionally used back roads to avoid tolls. He stopped for gas twice and went through several drive-thru's.

At about 11 am on Election Day, he crossed the Third Avenue Bridge into Manhattan, to avoid having to go through a tollbooth.

He drove across Manhattan to the west side and parked on 92nd Street, near a park between Riverside Drive and the West Side Highway. It was a beautiful fall day and he decided to go for a walk. He put on a baseball cap and some sunglasses and walked over to the pathway along the Hudson River.

There were runners and bikers and other walkers all around him. He smiled as people passed him.

Forty-five minutes later, as he walked back to his car he turned Miller's phone back on and dialed Sarah's number. It was Election Day. She wouldn't be in school, if she was still teaching. After three rings, she answered. He hadn't heard her voice in months.

"Hello."

He paused and led with the first words he ever said to her. "Um, hi."

She gasped, hearing his voice.

"Greg? Is it really you?"

"Yes."

"Where are you? How are you? You've been shot?"

Her voice broke him. After all he had done, after all of his mistakes and after all the people he had killed, he heard only love in her voice. He could hardly speak.

"Where are you?"

Finally he said, "Not far."

"Come home."

"I can't. It's too late."

"It's not. Come home. Come in. We can…"

"I'm sorry, Sarah. It was all me. Jane's death, everything was my fault. I've tried to make it mean something, but it is all my fault."

"It's not, Greg. Just come home. We can do something…"

"I can't come home. I love you, Sarah."

Chapter 113

The agents monitoring Sarah's calls couldn't believe their ears. Hopper was on the phone, talking to her from Miller's cell phone.

They called Agent Ready and used every resource available to track the call, but Hopper powered down the phone before they could pinpoint his location. Now they would have to wait to discover the location of the cell tower the phone had accessed.

Chapter 114

Greg hung up, turned off the phone and tossed it into a trashcan. He walked a few blocks north then got back in his car and drove up the West Side Highway, towards the Henry Hudson Bridge.

Chapter 115

Tony Frost, a homeless man who spent his days on the Upper West Side, saw a man toss what appeared to be a cell phone into a garbage can on the corner of Riverside Drive and 93rd Street. As soon as the man was out of sight, Frost retrieved the phone. He also found five returnable bottles and cans. He put them into the satchel he carried over his shoulder.

He walked a few blocks along Riverside, then turned into the little park between Riverside and the West Side Highway and found a bench. Frost rummaged through his satchel, counting the cans and bottles he had collected. He had twenty-three: $1.15. With that and the money he thought he could get for the phone, he might have a fun night ahead of him.

He took the phone from his pocket and turned it on, hoping it would work.

It immediately buzzed.

Frost answered it and heard a man's voice.

"Mr. Hopper?"

He clicked the "end" button to disconnect the call, but left the phone on.

Chapter 116

The agents monitoring Sarah's calls and Miller's phone called Ready as soon as the phone went back on.

"He's on the Upper West Side. We have his signal at 91st and Riverside, heading south."

Within minutes, police were all over the streets looking for him. They tracked the phone to a small park on 91st Street. Four officers sprinted into the park. They found a bald, belligerent, homeless man with the phone. He claimed he found it in a trashcan. Hopper apparently dumped it, but didn't bother to destroy it. The homeless man described the man who tossed it and said he thought the guy was heading north. Three of the officers took off in that direction while the fourth stayed with Frost and the phone.

Ready dispatched every resource he could to the area. Officers and available agents were sent to subway stations, roads, bridges, tunnels and were stopping pedestrians on sidewalks, looking every man and woman in the eye, questioning anyone who could possibly be Hopper.

Chapter 117

Greg was a few minutes ahead of the authorities as he approached the Henry Hudson Bridge. The bridge, which spans the Spuyten Duyvil Creek and the Harlem River, is about one hundred and fifty feet above the water. Everyone who crosses it has a breathtaking view of the Hudson River.

As he approached the toll plaza, he saw two police cars coming up behind him, about ten cars back. He drove through the automated tollbooth onto the upper tier of the bridge, which is exclusively for northbound traffic, out of Manhattan to Riverdale and the Bronx.

He stayed in the left lane. When he was about halfway across, he stopped his car. He put it in park and turned off the engine. The New York drivers behind him started to honk and scream with anger that boiled just beneath the surface.

Greg opened his door and walked three feet to the guardrail. He had been under so much pressure for so long. He had considered waiting for the election results, but knew there was nothing more he could do. He climbed up the rail and jumped off.

Chapter 118

Turnout for the mid-term election was lower than anyone expected. Only forty-one percent of eligible voters bothered to go to the polls. Eight incumbent senators lost their seats. Ninety-one incumbent congressmen lost.

The nation's apathy was palpable.

Chapter 119

Nineteen months later on June 9th, 2016, Mike Williams, the reporter for *The Erie Star* who first broke the Hopper story, walked to his desk. Things had calmed down considerably for Mike and his boss since the election. And then, as he was reading through his mail, he opened a letter from Florida.

Dear Mr. Williams,

In five months, we will be holding our first national election since the death of Greg Hopper. In the time since his death, nothing has changed. Congressional approval ratings remain near all time lows. There has been no new gun control legislation and there is no real talk of implementing term limits. Our national indifference has led incumbents to believe that they can continue to get away with the same selfish behavior that has served them so well in the past.

It may take longer than Mr. Hopper thought, but it is still time for change. So I am going to take over where Mr. Hopper left off. I am going to murder family members of congressmen and congresswomen seeking re-election after three or more terms and senators seeking re-election.

It is time to throw these bums out.

To show that I am serious, tonight after I mail this letter, I will murder the wife of Congressman David Sanford of Florida. She is the congressman's twenty-six year old second wife and a former member of his staff. Sanford left his wife and children to marry her. THROW THE INCUMBENTS OUT. VOTE FOR ANYONE ELSE. DEMAND TERM LIMITS

Williams looked at the postmark on the letter. It was from Florida and dated June 6th. The new Mrs. Sanford had been murdered on the

6th at approximately 11:15 pm, long after the post office closed. Her death had led the evening news the next night. She'd been tossed from the balcony of her high-rise apartment.

Steve Powell is a retired bond trader. He has degrees in finance from Miami University in Oxford, Ohio and the Wharton School at the University of Pennsylvania. Steve is an avid runner and a struggling but optimistic golfer. He is married with four grown sons and lives in Connecticut where he owns a small gym and writes.

If you liked this book,
like Steve Powell on *Facebook*
and follow him on *Twitter*
@StevePowell025
or check out his website

www.stevepowellbooks.com